S0-AWC-638

MORE MYSTERIES FROM THE BERKLEY PUBLISHING GROUP . . .

JENNY McKAY MYSTERIES: This TV reporter finds out where, when, why . . . *and* whodunit. "A more streetwise version of television's Murphy Brown."

—*Booklist*

by Dick Belsky
BROADCAST CLUES   LIVE FROM NEW YORK
THE MOURNING SHOW

CAT CALIBAN MYSTERIES: She was married for thirty-eight years. Raised three kids. Compared to that, tracking down killers is easy . . .

by D. B. Borton
ONE FOR THE MONEY   TWO POINTS FOR MURDER
THREE IS A CROWD

KATE JASPER MYSTERIES: Even in sunny California, there are cold-blooded killers . . . "This series is a treasure!"   —Carolyn G. Hart

by Jaqueline Girdner
ADJUSTED TO DEATH   MURDER MOST MELLOW
THE LAST RESORT   FAT-FREE AND FATAL
TEA-TOTALLY DEAD

FREDDIE O'NEAL, P.I., MYSTERIES: You can bet that this appealing Reno private investigator will get her man . . . "A winner." —Linda Grant

by Catherine Dain
LAY IT ON THE LINE   SING A SONG OF DEATH
WALK A CROOKED MILE   LAMENT FOR A DEAD COWBOY
BET AGAINST THE HOUSE

CALEY BURKE, P.I., MYSTERIES: This California private investigator has a brand-new license, a gun in her purse, and a knack for solving even the trickiest cases!

by Bridget McKenna
MURDER BEACH   DEAD AHEAD
CAUGHT DEAD

CHINA BAYLES MYSTERIES: She left the big city to run an herb shop in Pecan Springs, Texas. But murder can happen anywhere . . . "A wonderful character!"—*Mostly Murder*

by Susan Wittig Albert
THYME OF DEATH   WITCHES' BANE

LIZ WAREHAM MYSTERIES: In the world of public relations, crime can be a real career-killer . . . "Readers will enjoy feisty Liz!" —*Publishers Weekly*

by Carol Brennan
HEADHUNT   FULL COMMISSON

BET AGAINST THE HOUSE

CATHERINE DAIN

BERKLEY PRIME CRIME, NEW YORK

BET AGAINST THE HOUSE

A Berkley Prime Crime Book / published by arrangement with the author

PRINTING HISTORY
Berkley Prime Crime edition / February 1995

ISBN: 0-425-14580-8

Berkley Prime Crime Books are published by
The Berkley Publishing Group,
200 Madison Avenue, New York, NY 10016.
The name BERKLEY PRIME CRIME and the BERKLEY PRIME CRIME
design are trademarks belonging to Berkley Publishing Corporation.

PRINTED IN THE UNITED STATES OF AMERICA

10 9 8 7 6 5 4 3 2 1

BET AGAINST
THE HOUSE

▼

Chapter
1

"YOU EITHER HAVE it—or you've had it!" the woman with the microphone shouted. "And I've got it! It's Glory's turn!"

With that, she launched into an a cappella version of "Rose's Turn" from *Gypsy*, lyrics rewritten for the occasion. Ethel Merman couldn't have been more exuberant. Or more off key.

"This is why I asked you to meet me here," the young woman standing next to me whispered, shielding her mouth with her program. "I had to make sure you understood. There must be something you can dig up that will stop her."

"Are you sure you want to do this?" I held up my own program for the same purpose. "She's still your mother."

"I don't care. This is all so unpleasant."

Everything about the day, except for the woman on the platform, belied her words. The sun was shining, as it must for Graduation Day, but not blazing. The quad was a verdant background for the rows of professors in their medieval splendor, black robes with brightly colored hoods attached to indicate their colleges and disciplines, heads topped with tasseled mortarboards. Some of the robes were trimmed in black velvet, a regal touch that seemed a silent argument for a time when university professors were held in high esteem.

Behind them, students in plain, untrimmed black robes, rented for the day's ceremony, waited restlessly for the culmination of four years of hard play. Some of them may have studied. But if many of them had, the university had changed since my time.

Gloria Scope had just been awarded an honorary degree, in recognition of her contributions to the university over the years, and her late husband's contributions as well. She had started by giving a standard pep talk on seeing obstacles as challenges, referring obliquely to her problems with her children in the process. Now she was strutting back and forth on the platform, singing with raucous abandon. I could see why her daughter was embarrassed.

Some of the tassels in the front rows were starting to bob, so Tella wasn't the only one embarrassed. The robed wonders on the platform were looking at their feet, looking at each other, looking everywhere except at the spectacle in front of them. Professor Hellman, who had been my history teacher, stood out in his Harvard crimson robe. He was hiding his face in his hand. The statue of John Mackay bore the closest thing to a smile in sight.

I didn't like the idea of being paid by her daughter to dig up dirt on Gloria, but if Gloria had wanted good relations with her kids, she should have named them more carefully. If my name were Tella Scope, I might hate my mother, too. The boys were called Mike and Guy, but there was nothing one could do with Tella.

Gloria hushed the hopeful applause with one upraised hand and swung into an encore. She and Tella each had style, but they weren't ones you'd expect to find in the same household. For one thing, Gloria was loud. She was also short and stout. The robe made her look like a black fireplug. The gray hair frizzing out around the mortarboard reminded me of one of the Marx Brothers.

Tella was tall and fine boned, with a swan's grace, her body draped with a long white jacket over a burgundy silk camisole and white skirt. Her short blond hair had been sculpted so that it curved around her ears without an errant strand. A slender gold chain and small gold hoop earrings were her only adornments. And her voice was well modulated. I had trouble imagining her losing her temper.

We were standing in the shade of one of the many trees that made the Reno campus a springtime treasure. I had received an "A" in Victorian literature—a feat deemed impossible by the common lack of wisdom of my fellow undergraduates—by taking it one summer when I could read the novels the way they were meant to be read, sitting on the grass and leaning against a tree for a whole, lazy afternoon. And another. And another. And another. Ten years later I had remembered the trees better than the books.

Gloria had evidently written just the two choruses to "Rose's Turn," because she bowed at last to the desperately applauding audience and sat down. The university president came to the lectern and adjusted the microphone.

"Come on," Tella said. "We can talk somewhere else."

I left with a tug of regret. Gloria's speech was the last one, and it would have been fun to listen while the names of the graduates were called. The practice of actually handing out diplomas depended on small numbers, and UNR had finally become too big to let the departing seniors walk across the stage. But Tella was paying, and I had to hear what she wanted to say.

We worked through the crowd of parents and other assorted friends and relatives, out of the quad, past the School of Business, and across another sweep of lawn to the

Student Union. The cafeteria in the basement was open. We skipped the empty steam table, the few sandwiches of stale Wonder bread in Saran Wrap, and picked up two cups of coffee. Tella paid, and we took them to a table outside, overlooking more trees and Manzanita Lake, which was not much more than a large pond with swans. Even that close to real ones, the image of Tella as swanlike held.

An obese golden Labrador waddled over, looking hopeful.

"How much do you know about my family?" Tella asked.

"Only what I've read in the newspapers," I answered.

She grimaced, distorting the perfectly made-up face.

"Go on."

"Your father was Ted Scope, shortened from Scopelowski. He was a self-made millionaire, but he had to do it more than once. Started a computer company, lost it, started another one, hit big. When he died last year, he left his stock in Scope Chips and everything else to your mother. You and your brothers sued to break the will, and the lawsuit is still winding its way through the courts." I shrugged. "It must be tough, but I'm not sure what you want from me."

"I want—*we* want, my brothers know I'm doing this—I want you to find out something about her that we can use to force her to bargain."

The Labrador pushed his fat, wet nose against my leg. I reached down and patted his head. He settled it on my knee, looking up with desperate brown eyes. Tella and I were the only people on the terrace. Everyone else was at the ceremony, or already gone for the break. The dog had a lean couple of weeks ahead, until the summer session started.

"You want to blackmail your mother," I said.

Tella shifted uncomfortably and looked out at the swans.

"What makes you think there's something to find?"

"There has to be, there just has to be. She worked in a casino, for God's sake. Her past can't possibly stand up to scrutiny."

"A casino?"

"She was a twenty-one dealer when my father met her." Tella said "twenty-one" as if it were a social disease. I patted the dog again, not wanting to laugh. A flurry of fat brown sparrows landed on the next table, suddenly discovering that the terrace was inhabited.

"That isn't a crime. A lot of very nice women deal twenty-one. I'm willing to ask a few questions, but I think it's going to be a waste of your money." I didn't like the idea of getting involved in a family squabble, but Tella wasn't the type to write bad checks, and I needed the money. "Why can't somebody negotiate this? How did it get so nasty?"

"It started when my father was still alive. He took all the credit for Scope Chips, but the breakthrough in technology—the fuzzy-logic chip—was really my brother Mike's work. And Daddy treated Mike as if he were one more hired hand. Argued that the chip was a work-for-hire, didn't want Mike's name on the patent."

The Labrador had given up on me and was now staring woefully at Tella. She gave him a look in return that stopped him from even thinking about drooling on her white skirt. One sparrow hopped off the table and inspected the concrete.

"This so-called 'fuzzy-logic' chip. I have a sense of what fuzzy logic is—it's the gap between on and off. Somebody described it as the gradation between hairy and bald. But I don't understand the big deal. I thought the Japanese had been using fuzzy logic for years, to make fast trains come to a smooth stop, adjust heat in buildings, camera focus, things like that."

Tella nodded. "They have. But this is fuzzy logic in a microchip, fuzzy logic on the computer notebook level. That's the big deal. It's a second-generation expert system—a computer that learns. The first-generation computer notebooks couldn't do what they claimed, when it came to reading handwriting or anything else. This one can not only learn to recognize your handwriting, it can recognize your voice, too. You can teach it to recognize the command 'Take a letter,' for example. Dictate the letter and the computer prints it out, properly formatted."

"Technology eliminates secretaries in one fell swoop."

"Or frees them from the drudgery of dictation and transcription for more interesting and challenging tasks."

I could have pursued that argument, but it wouldn't have gotten us anywhere.

"So your brother figured it out, and your father took credit. Wasn't that the time to sue?"

"In retrospect, we probably should have had a showdown with him. But Mike was only nineteen when the patent process started, and at that time we all trusted Daddy to take care of us. By the time we began to wonder if he'd done the right thing for Mike, he had already had one heart attack, and we didn't want to be in a situation where we were pushing him into his coffin. Besides, it never occurred to any of us that he would leave everything to her."

"Nineteen? Mike was nineteen?"

"He's a genius," Tella said, so matter-of-factly that I couldn't question it.

"Had your father made anybody any promises?" If I wanted to inherit a company, I think it would have occurred to me to ask about arrangements.

The scout sparrow hopped back to the others. They conferred and flew away, noisily expressing disapproval.

"Not exactly. But Mike and I each had the title vice president, and all three of us were on the board of directors. Mom spent her life throwing parties. There wasn't a formal succession plan. Still, Mike and I had an informal one, and Daddy knew it."

"What was it?"

"Mike became head of research and I became CEO."

"And Guy?"

The Labrador had settled on the grass, far enough to be safe from Tella's glare, close enough to spot anything that might fall from the table. Two white swans slipped into the shade of a willow. Tella tapped her French-manicured acrylic nails against the table before she answered.

"Guy would continue to collect his salary as a board member, as well as his share of the distributions from the trust."

"According to the papers, he's a nut."

"Guy was missing for five days when he was eight years old. And he sincerely believes he spent those five days in a UFO. No one has come up with another explanation." She stopped watching the swans and turned to me, blue eyes held wide, as if to emphasize her sincerity. "Most of the time he functions normally. There have been moments, flashbacks—most obviously the time he went to a dentist and insisted on having his teeth pulled to get rid of what he said were implants in his fillings—but they're rare. That isn't why he doesn't have a more active decision-making role. He doesn't have one because he really doesn't want it. Mike and I include him in everything, and he trusts us. Truly."

I suppose every family has at least one.

"What did you think your father's will would say?"

"We knew there was a trust set up, and we knew our

mother was sole trustee and executor of the estate. What we didn't realize was the total control he gave her. And how she would decide to use it. When she walked into the first board meeting after he died, we thought it was a token appearance. We thought she was going to tell us how well we had been doing, tell us to carry on. Instead, she sat down in his chair at the head of the table, swiveled it around in a circle, and said, 'You know, I like it here.'" Tella shuddered at the memory.

"Then what?"

"Well, at first we thought we could work around her, but she started asking us all kinds of questions, second-guessing every tiny decision we made. Mike and I talked to the other members of the board, and we called another board meeting to give her our unanimous opinion. That she should go home. She looked around the table, left to right, and said, 'You're all fired.'"

I wasn't ready to admit it to Tella, but I was starting to like her mother.

"Did you stay fired?" I asked.

"No, of course not. While she either owns directly or controls almost forty percent of the company, she doesn't have the power to fire anyone. The board still operates, and Mike and I still have our jobs. But the family relationships have been tense. I don't need to tell you how difficult Christmas was."

She was right, she didn't need to. Besides, I'd had my own Christmas to contend with. All people with mothers do. Although I was actually getting along with mine fairly well.

"What's the status of the court case?"

"With the attorneys charging by the hour, and a contingency bonus for winning, I expect it to drag on for the rest of our lives. If she starts a proxy fight—which I fully expect her to do—another set of attorneys and investment bankers take a hunk of the corporate earnings."

"A proxy fight?"

"Asking shareholders, the public, to vote to fire the board and install a new one, one that will back her."

"Do you think they would?"

Tella sighed and shook her head. "Who knows. With the block she owns, she could do it by winning a couple of institutional fund managers over to her side. It's chancy. That's why I hired you."

"You want to short-circuit both the judicial system and the stock exchange," I said.

She frowned, then nodded. "It may not sound nice, but it's practical."

"Tell me about the other board members."

"There are three outside members—Tom Warfield, George Harding, and Ross Zabriskie. All Daddy's friends from the club."

I knew the names. They were in the newspapers often enough, for one reason or another. Tom Warfield had been a player in New York during the eighties, mergers and acquisitions. George Harding had sold a company that made circuit boards for the Sidewinder missile six months before the program was cut from the Pentagon budget. Ross Zabriskie was an expatriate Californian whose fast-food chain was now part of Taco Bell. They had each taken what appeared to be an early retirement in Reno, because they found both the Nevada lifestyle and the Nevada tax struc-ture amenable. They had all become respected members of the Reno community. But "club" didn't register.

I must have looked puzzled, because Tella added, "It's a club of millionaires. All male, all self-made. They own a hunting lodge in the Sierras, where they occasionally spend a weekend."

"Hunting?"

Tella laughed sharply. "No one ever comes back with a deer across the hood, if that's what you're asking. They drink, play poker, drink, talk business, and do guy stuff. Which sometimes includes women, but never wives. Mother always hated it, but she couldn't stop Daddy from going. Of course, she inherited his membership, along with everything else, because he didn't specifically leave it to anyone. Ironically, that has worked to Mike's and my advantage—I think it's the major reason the three others are backing us in our efforts to break the will."

I thought of Gloria storming the hunting lodge with a hatchet. I imagined those guys wanted to break the will a lot.

"With the outside board members on your side, with all their clout, and especially with Warfield's connections on Wall Street, it's hard to see how Gloria has much chance of winning. Searching for youthful indiscretions has to be gilding the lily," I said.

"We can win in the long run," Tella said patiently. "But in the long run—"

"We're all dead," I chimed in.

"Exactly."

"Well, after seeing her up on the stage doing a buck-and-wing in academic garb, and after what you've just said about the lineup against her, I can't imagine anything I could dig up that would convince her to negotiate. But if you want to go ahead, I'll do what I can."

"Good."

It wasn't, but I let it go.

"Where did she work, when did she work there, and what name was she using?"

"The Mother Lode, the early sixties, and Gloria Fry."

"Is there anything else you can give me? Did she belong to any organizations? Take classes? Does she have any old friends who don't like her?"

"She's never talked very much about who she was before she married my father. If I could come up with anything more, I'd tell it to you."

I had been paying more attention to the dog, the swans, and Tella than my coffee. I took a sip, but it had become tepid, and I wished I'd ordered a Coke instead.

"Was she born in Reno?"

"She was born in New York. She came to Reno to get a no-fault divorce, which wasn't available there. She met my father and stayed."

"Can you give me anything on her first husband? That's probably where I ought to look. And a New York PI might do a better job."

Tella started tapping her nails again.

"If you need help, get it. I'll pay for it. Her first husband was Larry Agnotti, and all I know is that she says he was a bum."

"Yeah. Women say that about first husbands."

Gloria and Ramona—my mother—should get together.

"Anything else?" Tella was watching the swans again, tired of my questions.

"Not right now. I'll start on what I have, and let you know if I need more information."

"Good." She held out her hand and shook mine firmly. "I was so pleased to find that there was a woman private investigator in Reno. I think women need to support each other's work, don't you?"

"Thanks for hiring me," I said, retrieving my hand.

I think people need to support good people. And I wasn't sure I was on the right side of this one.

Tella walked across the terrace and around the side of the building, where a concrete stairway would take her back to the main street of the campus. She couldn't be much over thirty, from what she said about the dates her mother worked in the clubs. But the hair, suit, and makeup helped her look close to forty. Staying young isn't an advantage to a woman running a company.

I knew from the newspapers that she was the oldest of the children. Mike and Guy were probably still in their twenties. Ted Scope made a judgment call putting their mother in charge, but I wasn't sure it was bad judgment. He also could have made one of his buddies executor and trustee if he had wanted to. I needed to find out more about the balance of power.

The Labrador came back for another try, liquid brown eyes begging me to find an uneaten crumb. I patted his head one last time, then followed Tella to the stairs. She had already disappeared.

Black robes dotted the lawn and the sidewalk when I emerged from the shadow of the Student Union. The ceremony had evidently just ended, and the crowd was dispersing. Professor Hellman—a standout in the crimson robe—was on his way into the humanities building, the one that used to have AGRICVLTVRE carved above the door, now covered with the word *Frandsen*. I cut across the lawn to intercept him.

"My God, Freddie O'Neal!" he exclaimed when I caught the sleeve of his gown just before he swept through the door. "I'm on my way to my office, to get out of this. Come with me."

I fell into step as he started down the wide, curving staircase to the basement. His office was the first one on the left, with a high window that provided an excellent view of grass and feet. The semester's clutter of papers was still spread across his desk and a table, and the bookshelves were in their usual disorder. The painting of *Danaë and the Shower of Gold*, which I had always liked, hung at its usual angle.

Professor Hellman took off his mortarboard and tossed it toward the table. His wispy gray hair stood on end, trying to go with the cap. He took off the crimson robe and hung it on the ancient oak coatrack next to the door. Underneath he had been wearing a plaid cotton shirt and cotton slacks. From the splendor of tradition to the commonplace, too suddenly.

He fell heavily into the leather chair behind his desk, took off his glasses, and rubbed his eyes. I sat down in one of the smaller chairs—a student chair—across from him.

"Terrible, just terrible. Did you see her?" he asked.

"I don't think I could have missed her, sir."

"This kowtowing for money is a disgrace. An honorary degree should recognize accomplishment, not the gift of inherited money." He dropped his hand and looked at me, his eyes unfocused and colorless without his glasses. "Not that we're any different from any other institution of higher learning. An almost total abandonment of historic values in the face of the struggle for economic survival."

"Is she giving a lot?" I asked.

"A new computer science laboratory and an endowed chair." He sighed and put his glasses back on. "We couldn't turn it down, of course."

"Did she ask for anything besides an honorary degree?"

"What do you mean?"

"Well, with the court case, her kids suing her, and a

possible proxy fight coming up, I just wondered if she might be looking for help."

Professor Hellman leaned back in his chair.

"I should have known you didn't stop by to reminisce about your school days. What's your interest in the Scopes?"

"I'm not sure yet." And that was the truth. There was a time when I would have made up a story to keep him talking, but I didn't feel like lying.

"It's a matter of public record that the university endowment fund—which is not extensive, since most of our funding comes from the state legislature—owns a block of Scope Chips, donated some years ago by the late Ted Scope. If she wanted to convince the regents of her competence, however, today's performance was miscalculated." He smiled gently, and I remembered how hard it had been to mine the dry wit from his lectures. "Of course, if the regents are both sufficiently calculating and sufficiently beloved of Dame Fortune, we could find ourselves the beneficiaries of the Warfield Chair of Finance, the Zabriskie Chair of Marketing, and the Harding Chair of Engineering. And the children may yet run the company."

"The papers say Guy's a nut, and Tella says Mike's a genius. She seems normal enough, but maybe that's only in relation to the others. Did you know their father?"

Professor Hellman shook his head.

"Only by reputation. But if the rumors even approached accuracy, Ted Scope was both a genius and, as you so graphically put it, a nut. The children can therefore claim both genius and madness as their inheritance, whatever the dispute about more tangible legacies."

"Lucky them." I wasn't feeling any better about working for Tella, but the check she had given me before the graduation ceremony began was beginning to burn a hole in my pocket. I stood up and held out my hand. "I won't take any more of your time. It was good to see you again."

"Yes," he said, rising and returning the handshake. "Please stop by when you aren't working on a case, especially if you want to discuss the advisability of attending graduate school. You'll need a second career, you know. You can't be a private investigator forever."

"I'll think about it, sir. But not this year."

My smile stayed until I got out the door and started up the stairs. I wasn't sure why he thought I'd need a second career, particularly when I was feeling young enough to do this one forever. Skip-trace work—which is most of my business—isn't like football or tennis. You're not over the hill at thirty-three.

I had parked my Jeep on Sierra Street, a block west and a couple of blocks south of the campus, because on-campus parking is chancy even without a commencement exercise, and I didn't want to deal with the crowds. My conversation with Professor Hellman had taken just enough time for gridlock to form on the main drag.

As I headed down the tree-lined sidewalk toward the pillars that marked the exit, I spotted a black fireplug with frizzy gray hair bobbing along about half a block away. I picked up my pace, wanting to get a closer look.

The fat golden Labrador, who had also been wandering toward the pillars, evidently resigned to a diet of whatever happened to be in his dish at home, spotted her, too, his last great hope for the afternoon. He planted himself, firmly if woefully, in her path.

"Who the hell are you?" she asked the dog in a voice slightly hoarse from her on-stage triumph.

He whimpered that he was dying of starvation.

"Yeah, yeah. I suppose that collar doesn't mean a thing. You were abandoned weeks ago."

By this time I was only a few feet behind them, and I could see his face perk up and his tail start to wag in anticipation of a possible treat. Just as she bent over to pet him, something whizzed past my shoulder and I heard the crack and echo of a rifle.

"Get down!" I shouted.

I lunged for her, and the three of us went over in a tangle of black cotton. A small branch crashed to the lawn, a victim of a second shot. The dog started barking frantically, trying to disentangle himself.

Gloria Scope rolled over and sat up, hatless and wild-eyed.

"Jesus," she said. "You saved my life."

Chapter 2

"SO WHAT DID the Man say?" Deke asked as he cut himself another hunk of steak.

I had spent the afternoon with Gloria and the police, endured a brief conversation with the police beat reporter for the *Herald*, and by sundown I was looking for food and more amiable company. Deacon Adams, former Air Force survival instructor, now security guard and occasional cat-sitter, was ensconced in his usual stool at the counter of the Mother Lode coffee shop when I got there. I ordered a hamburger and beer, filled out a Keno ticket, and told him the story.

"Not a lot, or at least not a lot to me. Matthews got the case, and he wanted to know what I was doing there. I told him I'd been chatting with Professor Hellman, and he didn't push it. The angle of the bullets indicates the sniper was probably in the Morrill Hall tower. And with all the robes, smuggling a rifle on and off campus would have been easy."

"Does Mrs. Scope have any ideas about who might want her dead?"

"I think 'Who doesn't?' might be an easier question to answer." I waved my empty beer bottle at Diane, the waitress at our station. She nodded and brought me another one. "Whoever-it-was wasn't a pro. A pro would have hit her."

"Unless he just wanted to scare her," Deke said. At least, I think that's what he said through a mouthful of fries.

"I thought of that. Not so far from blackmail to firing a couple of shots, although I don't think it was Tella who fired them. For one thing, she wasn't wearing a robe, and a woman in white carrying a rifle would have been spotted. But it might have been one of the other parties to the lawsuit. And Matthews reads the papers. I'm sure he'll check everybody out. In any case, Gloria's taking it seriously, and she's right to do that. She wanted to hire me as a bodyguard. I said no."

"Good move. That might be construed as conflict of interest."

I waited while the Keno numbers came up, then pulled out another dollar to replay my card.

"Only if I cash her daughter's check, which I haven't."

"You lose one more Keno card and you'll have to cash the check to pay for your dinner."

I glared at him and flagged down the runner.

"That's part of it, but the rest is that I didn't do too well last time I was a bodyguard."

"It might be you should work for the mother, then. Get back on the horse that threw you."

"Yeah, I knew you'd say that."

The Keno runner, who had looked young when she took the job two years earlier, nodded in recognition when she took my dollar and moved on.

"I know you can't afford to turn them both down. I'd say you can't afford to turn down either one, except for that conflict of interest." He had cleaned his plate of everything but the parsley. Diane was there to pick it up before he had a chance to push it away.

"How about pie?" she asked.

"I'm getting too fat for pie." Deke sighed as he said it. He had been gaining weight, and all of it was settling around his middle. Ever since I've known him, he's had that former athlete heft, the adipose-coated muscles, but this time he was looking a little soft. His face had always reminded me of eggplant, but now the jowls were threatening to swallow everything from his receding hairline to his collarbone.

Diane didn't ask a second time.

"I don't want to be Gloria Scope's bodyguard, Deke. And I already told her daughter that I didn't think I'd find anything useful in her past, and I meant it. Tella still gave me the go-ahead. My guess is that what happened this afternoon isn't going to shake either mother or daughter enough for one of them to quit." I paused to contemplate the label on my beer bottle. "I think I can earn Tella's money with a clear conscience. And without interfering in an ongoing police investigation into who took a shot at Gloria, which was another consideration."

"Then why are we having this conversation?"

"Because I don't know what I'll do if I'm wrong, and I do find something."

Deke fixed me with his small, red-rimmed eyes.

"Best you find out, then."

"Yeah. Well, then, let's start. Do you know anybody who's worked here since the sixties? Or who retired from the casino but might remember Gloria? She's been in the spotlight enough that she'd be hard to forget."

"I'll have to check around. Might be a couple of old-timers who could help."

"Thanks."

I finished my beer, lost another Keno game, and we went our separate ways, Deke to get ready for work, me to walk home via the video rental outlet.

I looked for something with a good family conflict, but there hadn't been any remakes of the *Oresteia* recently. I settled for *Duel in the Sun*. The shoot-out between Gregory Peck and Jennifer Jones is my idea of sex and violence.

Butch and Sundance, my two long-haired tomcats, were waiting on the porch. I was lucky—they were still hungry. If I'm gone too long, they forage and leave the remains on my office carpet. They were a little freaked at the Labrador's scent clinging to my jeans, but they settled down when I headed for the kitchen. I opened a can of food for them and another beer for me.

There was one more thing to do before watching the movie. I belong to a computer network of independent private investigators who save each other wear and tear by doing odd jobs in other cities. I'd never asked anybody in New York for help, but I did have a colleague in Las Vegas, and I could bet he had contacts in New York. I booted up my computer and sent an E-mail message to Rudy Stapp, sketching in the basics, giving the names Gloria Scope, Gloria Fry, and Larry Agnotti.

I ignored messages on my answering machine from Tella, "News at Eleven," and my friend Sandra Herrick, a reporter for the *Herald*, who was truly annoyed that I hadn't called her while Gloria and I were waiting on campus for the police.

After *Duel in the Sun*, I caught part of a late movie on cable. This time the shoot-out was Burt Lancaster and Marie Gomez. But he didn't die.

The phone woke me up at the ungodly hour of seven-thirty in the morning.

"I hope I didn't wake you," Tella said. "Did you tell the police I hired you?"

I struggled upright and pushed the hair out of my face. Whatever happened to thanks-for-saving-my-mother's-life.

"Since I didn't think it had anything to do with the attack on your mother, I decided not to. I hope I was right. And I haven't deposited the check yet, so I could still change my mind."

"Please don't. I didn't have anything to do with the sniper. I do feel bad about that. And I'm glad you were there to save her." She stuck it in as if suddenly conscious of its absence. "I want her to quit—I want her to go back to the party circuit, where she belongs—but I wouldn't hire someone to shoot her. Besides, if someone is willing to kill her to stop her, it's even more important that we have some ammunition"—Tella stumbled over that—"nonlethal, of course—to convince her to step down."

"You are underestimating your mother and wasting your money." I had to say that, and promised myself it would be my last protest. "If a sniper won't stop her, she won't quit as long as she's alive."

"Try. Please try."

Better me than someone else.

"I've already started a couple of lines of inquiry, and I'll keep them open."

"Thank you. She's going to call you this morning."

"What? Your mother?"

Butch had left the bed when the phone rang. Sundance had hung in until my voice got loud, but he, too, decided there had to be a better place to sleep. He glared at me and hopped down.

"Yes. My mother. I didn't mention it yesterday, but another project of hers is a new musical comedy, and she's holding a sing-through tonight at the Reno Theatrical Society to try to bring some other investors."

"Investors for what? The Reno Theatrical Society is an amateur group."

"Well, she wants to take the show to Broadway. She could do it alone, of course, but she thinks it ought to be a community project."

"For God's sake, why?"

I think theater is okay, but if I were going to put my money into a community project, I could imagine a lot of others that would elbow it out of line.

"The musical is called *Oh, Nevada*," Tella said. "My mother thinks it would be good for the state."

"Come on. Somebody saw the revival of *Oklahoma!* last year and got big ideas. I'll tell your mother I'm busy."

"No, don't do that. This will give you an opportunity to meet my brothers and the outside members of the board, all in one spot. I think you ought to come. You seem to have some doubts about what we're doing, and meeting everyone will help. These will be billable hours."

Tella had said the magic words.

"Okay. If your mother invites me, I'll be there. You have to understand, though, that the incident yesterday means that the police may also be hanging around your mother, and I'm not going to do anything to interfere in a police investigation."

"No problem. See you tonight."

"One more thing. Your mother wanted to hire me as a bodyguard. I told her no—but I didn't tell her it would be a conflict of interest. At some point she may have to know you've hired me. Think about telling her."

Tella was silent for a moment.

"I'll think about it."

She hung up before I could say anything more.

I really wanted to go back to sleep, but the phone call had left me in that half-awake state that isn't as comforting as sleep and isn't as productive as alertness, but effectively rules out either. I wandered to the kitchen to microwave some instant coffee.

Three hours later I was sorting papers on my desk, trying to figure out which files were open, which were closed, and what I should be collecting money for, when the phone rang again.

"I want to thank you one more time for saving my life," Gloria Scope said. "You were really heroic yesterday. Do they say that about women?"

"Why not? And you're welcome."

"Have you changed your mind about being my bodyguard? I hope so."

"No. I'm sorry, but I don't do that kind of work, or at least not very well. There are a lot of people who do, though, and you shouldn't have any trouble finding someone."

"Yeah, but I like you."

I felt a terrible twinge of guilt when she said that. The worst of it was, I liked her, too.

"Anyway, I had another reason for calling," Gloria continued. "I want to invite you to a show tonight, at the Reno Theatrical Society. A preview of a new musical about Nevada. I meant to invite you yesterday, after we talked to the police, but I forgot. It's at eight-thirty, dress casual."

"Thanks. I'll be there. And casual dress is all I have."

"You're tall and you have long legs. You look good in pants. I've always envied women who looked good in pants. Besides, with all that gorgeous hair you don't need to think about clothes."

One more tug at my heartstrings.

"Thanks again," I said.

"There's a party after the show, at the house, and you're also invited to that. You can pick up directions at the theater. And bring a friend if you want to."

"I'll be alone, if that's all right."

"Sure. You aren't seeing anybody? Is that it?"

I didn't know what to say, but she leaped in again anyway.

"It's none of my business, and I'm sorry if I sounded pushy. Come alone, and let me think about who I know."

I still didn't know what to say.

"About the bodyguard job—" I began.

"Yes?"

I couldn't do it.

"My best guess is that you'll be okay as long as you stay in a crowd, that whoever took a shot at you yesterday isn't going to self-destruct by doing something in public. But I think you ought to hire somebody, Mrs. Scope, I really do."

"Yeah, okay. And it's Gloria."

"Gloria. Thanks for inviting me. I'll see you tonight."

I checked the closet for something that could go to the theater and a party, knowing that what Gloria meant by casual probably wasn't quite what I meant. The best I could come up with was white jeans and a jacket with a brown silk blouse. I had gotten my hair trimmed before going to graduation, so the ends weren't ragged. I could leave it loose, not pull it into a ponytail.

I looked at myself in the mirror, blond hair, darker eyebrows, freckles, square jaw, and wondered if I ought to buy a lipstick. And then I was embarrassed at the thought.

Or rather, for the reason behind the thought.

Which was that Gloria was going to try to set me up with

somebody, and I hadn't stopped her, and I didn't want either one of us, Gloria or me, to look foolish.

You'd think that having somebody around for just a couple of months, after having been alone for years, wouldn't change a person much. Or I would have thought that, anyway. But I hadn't been lonely before—at least I hadn't been aware of feelings that I would have called loneliness. Ever since I'd come back from Elko, though, I'd been lonely.

And I didn't know what to do about it.

On top of that, the short relationship that had never quite come together with Sam Courter hadn't left me feeling confident about my ability to run out there and try again. Not that I'd felt exactly confident before.

Hell. I was going to do my job, and Gloria probably wasn't going to find a guy to introduce me to—I cringed at the thought of being set up—on such short notice anyway.

So I didn't run out and buy lipstick. I went as me, unadorned.

The small brick building that housed the Reno Theatrical Society was on Sierra Street, not far from the university. The parking lot was too small for the crowd, and I had to drive three blocks farther up the hill to find a spot, even though I was a half hour early.

Small groups of people were eddying on the sidewalk, some smoking a last cigarette before going in. I was right about different ideas of casual—almost everybody was wearing a suit. Casual meant less than black tie to this crowd. There were a few couples in Western chic, but they were the exceptions. I spotted three or four political faces, familiar from TV news, chatting with faces familiar from the newspaper's society pages. Trying to come up with their names didn't seem worthwhile.

I eased my way between backs and shoulders and up the concrete steps. The heavy old wood doors were propped open, exposing a lobby jammed with people. The box office counter was stacked with programs and something that turned out to be a prospectus for investors, including the production plans for tryouts in San Francisco and Los Angeles before going to New York. Nobody was behind the counter handing out tickets, and I wished I had asked Gloria for more information about seating.

"There you are."

A hand grabbed my elbow, and I looked down to see Gloria Scope standing next to me, in nobody's idea of casual attire. She was wearing a black silk ball gown, nineteenth-century style, with a hoopskirt that ballooned at two odd angles because of the press of the crowd. Diamonds nestled in her frizzy hair, dangled from her ears, and drizzled down her exposed chest. She had an almost uncanny resemblance to photographs of Eilley Orrum, one of the discoverers of the Comstock Lode, and hence a founder of Virginia City.

"You look fantastic," I said. And that was the truth.

She beamed at me. "I'm going to make a speech at the end of the show—just a short one—but I wanted to look like one of the cast." The hand on my elbow guided me toward the door to the auditorium. "I've reserved a few seats for family, and one is for you."

I didn't count the rows and I hadn't counted the crowd, but it looked to me as we started down the aisle as if the lobby horde would end up playing musical chairs. A scattering of invitees already dotted the seats, with more than enough outside to fill the rest.

Ten vacant seats about a third of the way down had white "Reserved" signs on them, and Gloria stopped at that row.

"Best seats in the house," she said. "Close enough to see

everything, far enough back so that nobody spits on you hitting a high note."

"Your children are going to be here, too?" I asked, still not sure how this was going to work.

"The entire board of Scope Chips will be here," Gloria said, looking up at me with innocent brown eyes. "How can we work it out if we can't be polite to each other?"

I took the pudgy hand that was firmly gripping my elbow.

"I don't know, Gloria, but I hope you find a way."

"Have a seat." She patted my hand. "The others will be along soon. I'll be watching the show from backstage, so I'll see you later."

She walked back up the narrow aisle, her hoopskirt forcing people coming down to squeeze against the chairs on either side. If I ever again doubted twentieth-century progress, I would remind myself of the hoopskirt.

Since I was the first of the group to be seated, I had one more small dilemma. Did I take the aisle seat, so that I could stretch my legs comfortably but everyone would have to climb over me, or did I sit politely but miserably in the center? A rising feeling of claustrophobia tilted the choice to the aisle seat.

The tide flowed down the aisles, into the seats of the small auditorium. The building was strangely without character for an amateur theatrical group that had kept going for close to half a century. White walls dotted with torchy sconces, dark red movie-theater seats, and a dark red curtain behind a simple proscenium arch. That was it.

Three couples paused in the aisle next to me, waiting for me to do something about my legs. All six were tall and attractive, with the ageless look that over-forty people of a certain affluence seem to acquire as a birthright. The three men were in blue-gray suits, the three women in muted silks. I stood, flipping my seat up, to let them pass. They didn't introduce themselves.

I glanced around, avoiding staring at the passing backs, and spotted Sandra Herrick with her husband, Don Echeverria, sitting on the other side of the theater a few rows up. She made a face at me, and I remembered that I hadn't returned her call. I wasn't surprised she was there—her father, Bud Herrick, had been the artistic director of the Reno Theatrical Society for as long as I could remember. He was probably backstage with Gloria.

The three couples sat all the way in, leaving three empty seats next to me.

Just as the sconces began to dim, Tella Scope and two young men with thin dark hair and pasty faces, so much alike they could have been twins, plummeted into the vacant seats. They both had Gloria's round face. The small dark eyes, slightly out of focus, didn't look like either Gloria's or Tella's. Neither brother had a hint of Tella's grace.

Tella was dressed in a flowing navy blue silk pantsuit with a white blouse and more of the simple gold jewelry she had worn the day before. I imagined her with a drawer full of simple gold jewelry. Her brothers interpreted casual the way I did. They wore open-necked plaid shirts and cotton slacks. One topped his with a faded denim jacket, the other a brown leather bomber jacket.

Tella took the inside seat, and the brother with the bomber jacket ended up next to me. He smiled, and I knew he had to be Guy. The teeth were too white and too even to be real.

A spotlight hit the piano in what wasn't an orchestra pit, and the audience applauded as the pianist, a man with full white hair wearing a tux, slipped from behind the curtain and walked down the steps to his seat. The man waved and bowed, then started a rousing overture. The audience applauded again when the curtains parted to reveal a stage empty except for sic lecterns, and continued to applaud as six regulars of the RTS took their places, one man dressed as a stage manager, three men and two women in period costumes.

The stage manager narrated the action, the couple in the center played Eilley Orrum and Sandy Bowers, and the other three took multiple roles, both singing and speaking. It was a little confusing, but the audience was charitable and applauded a lot.

Oh, Nevada spanned the five years from 1859 to 1864, from the discovery of the Comstock Lode to statehood, mostly history book stuff, with the romance between Eilley Orrum and Sandy Bowers for a storyline. So much for Gloria's costume. In fact, Gloria looked more the part than the woman singing it, who was taller and prettier.

I did learn for the first time—if it was even true—that Eilley Orrum had made decisions by consulting a crystal ball that she had brought with her from Scotland. In any case, she had done well, getting half a supposedly worthless claim in exchange for an unpaid laundry bill, marrying the muleskinner who had the other half of the claim, Sandy Bowers, and then becoming fabulously wealthy. The musical skipped her divorce from her first husband and her early claim to independence, which I thought was sort of a shame.

The songs were the kind that sound okay when you're listening to them but you can't remember afterward. A couple of them might have been better with full orchestra and chorus, production values, all that, but I'm no judge. I was getting restless before the intermission.

When the lights came up after the wedding scene that ended the first act, I would have headed straight out to the street, but I had to say hello to Tella, who had to introduce me to Mike and Guy. That meant we caught the crowd, moving slowly and uncomfortably out for the break, with nothing to say to one another.

Sandra was waiting in the lobby, poised so that everybody could get past her, but close enough to grab.

"I'm sorry," I said. "I should have called you."

"It would have been the thoughtful, friendly thing to do."

Sandra was wearing a Chinese red dress that would have looked great on television. Sandra would always look great on television, especially with her blond hair and peaches-and-cream skin, but she had opted off camera and into print because she had wanted the time to research and write more thoughtful material. That, and the television station hadn't been nice about her pregnancy. Their loss.

"I'm sorry," I said again. "The police beat reporter got everything I had to say about the attack on Gloria Scope, and it didn't occur to me that anyone but Ramona would be concerned."

I hadn't called Ramona, either, but I didn't mention that. As I thought about it, however, I was surprised she hadn't called me.

"What were you doing there in the first place?"

"A client invited me to graduation."

"Did you see Gloria's performance?" Sandra whispered that discreetly, even though everyone in the lobby had certainly heard about it, and we were too packed for privacy.

Nobody turned to stare. Yesterday's news.

"I did. It wasn't grounds for murder."

Sandra shook her head.

"If that isn't, this is."

"Come on. It's historical myth, and the natives will love it."

"The Native Americans won't. I'm surprised there aren't

pickets. One more reference to 'savages' and I'll leave in protest."

"I'm waiting for somebody to say, 'The only good Injun is a dead Injun.' Don't take it so seriously."

"Suppose somebody said that about women?"

"That would be different," I admitted. "I can only stand to watch somebody else's ox gored. I confess I'm grateful that I don't have to watch the chorus line of Julia Bulette and her Happy Hookers. And I don't want to be lectured about it."

"As long as you realize an ox is being gored, that's the best I can hope for." Sandra sighed to let me know how hopeless she thought I was.

The lobby lights blinked to signal the end of the intermission. People started flowing back toward the auditorium. I caught Sandra's arm as the three handsome couples shouldered past.

She raised her eyebrows, then followed their passage with wide blue eyes.

"Lunch tomorrow?" she asked.

"See you then," I said.

"By the way. I like your hair."

I muttered a word of thanks and went back to my seat.

The first act was Eilley Orrum's rise, the second her fall. The mining claim was exhausted, Sandy Bowers dead, and she almost lost the house. Only after Sandy Bowers spoke to her through the crystal ball did she manage to pull it all together and save the estate by opening it to the public.

I was already nervous when Gloria walked onstage at the end, even before the applause died and she opened her mouth.

"When I agreed to back *Oh, Nevada*," she began, "I didn't realize how prophetic it would be."

Gloria was savvy enough to wait for the ripple to die down before she continued.

"Yes." She raised her arms like Aimee Semple MacPherson. "Yes! Ted's spirit speaks to me! And he wants me to save his company!"

"It's a lie!"

Guy was on his feet, next to me, then scrambling to get across my legs. He ran down the aisle and up the stairs to the stage.

"It's a lie!" he panted. "I know it—Dad doesn't speak to her. I've seen him, and I know!"

"Close the curtains!" Gloria roared.

The curtains closed with a crash, and the house lights came up on the stunned audience.

Tella leaned across Mike and the empty seat.

"I hope you'll join us for the party," she said.

Chapter
3

"THEY SAY CHRYSLER was run that way for years—seances in the boardroom to evoke the ghost of Walter P., who would tell them what to do."

"Yes, and look what happened to Chrysler. Almost disappeared. Saved by Lee Iacocca and federal bailouts."

I couldn't see who was talking. They were behind me, a man and a woman, walking up the aisle, and I didn't want to turn around and look.

Tella had given me a map to the party, and then she and Mike had headed toward the stage to collect Guy. The rest of the audience slowly left their seats.

I caught Sandra and Don in the lobby.

"Are you guys going to the party?" I asked hopefully.

Sandra shook her head.

"Baby-sitter," she said.

"Sorry," Don added.

I didn't think he meant it.

"See you tomorrow," Sandra said as they were swept out the front door.

Walking the three blocks to my car gave me time to think, if not enough to sort anything out. I was feeling a bit more cautious about Gloria's ability to run the company. Not that she had ever struck me as the perfect businessperson. Still, I wasn't happy about blackmail, even if it was only the emotional sort.

When I had glanced at the map in the lobby, I realized I didn't need it. The Scopes lived in a house that had fascinated me as a child, built by one of the early gambling czars to resemble a castle on an acre of land near the edge of town. In the intervening fifty years, the city had swept past it on all sides.

I took Sierra straight down to California Street, then doglegged to Plumas. When I was a kid I had pestered my father to drive by the castle, even if we were just going to the grocery store and it was miles out of the way. Sometimes he said yes. More often than Ramona had. As an adult, I could see that the concrete towers soared over a rather ordinary brick base. The resemblance to a castle was superficial, and I was almost embarrassed to remember that I had imagined living there when I grew up. Nevertheless, I was glad to have a chance to see inside.

Two young men with red jackets and black bow ties were standing at the entrance to the driveway. I drove past them. I could park my own Jeep.

I had a long walk back on the pavement. There were no sidewalks, and the valets were parking the Cadillacs and the Lincolns perilously close to the hedge. Paint scratches on the passenger side were a hazard I had managed to avoid.

I nodded to the red jacket still on duty when I reached the corner. My boots crunched on the gravel driveway, and my heart had a sudden, childlike tilt as I reached the central turret, which held the front door, and touched the brass lion's-head knocker.

A pad with a ten-key layout had been drilled into the old brick to the right of the door. The modern equivalent of the moat. No light was flashing, so the security system wasn't on. The door wasn't even shut tight, because it opened from the pressure of my hand.

The narrow entryway, round as the turret, was overpowered by a Victorian hat rack and umbrella stand with hooks, knobs, and handles surrounding a cloudy mirror. It was otherwise empty—no one had graced it with so much as a parasol. I passed it and turned left into a large room where the party was already in full swing.

I couldn't spot either Tella or her mother, so I slid around the edge of the crowd toward the bar. The room seemed designed for parties, with all the furniture against the wall, arranged in conversation groups. There were too many people for me to see much more. And too many for me to get a good look at the art. I found myself so close to a fauve painting that I couldn't even see what it was. I thought it was a marina—it seemed to me a lot of fauve artists had been into boats—but at that range the primary colors had deconstructed into bright slashes and gray canvas, and I couldn't be sure. I was certain that it was an original, and it was expensive. So were several other paintings that I was too close to appreciate.

Voices were politely muted, but I still caught snatches of conversation. Nobody was talking about investing in the show, and at least one man was thinking of selling his shares in Scope Chips.

"Not now," the man beside him argued. "In a battle for control, you want to hold out for the highest bidder. My bet's on Warfield to support the kids only until the will is overturned, then raise the money for a leveraged buyout, a hostile one if necessary. He won't take a backseat to the mother or the daughter, either one."

"I'd agree, except that the major asset of the company is

the smart son. How does he get rid of the girl and the crazy son and keep the smart one?"

Somebody's elbow hit me in the back, and I missed the answer.

The two men behind the bar were wearing red vests and black bow ties. I asked one for a beer, and when pressed for a brand, took Bud. I buy American, I drink American.

A couple of people near the door started to applaud, and others picked it up. I could see the tip of some black feathers, about shoulder high to the crowd, and figured Gloria was making her entrance.

Going to a party where I don't know anybody is one of those rash acts that I commit from time to time and never understand afterward. I was already wishing I had begged off. I had nobody to talk to and didn't feel like winding back through the throng to Gloria, who had plenty of people to talk to. Just as I decided to put down my beer and leave, Tella appeared at my side.

"I can't stay," she said. She sipped from a champagne flute and checked the crowd as she talked, wide blue eyes filing every face in memory. "Guy is distraught, and I'm going to have to sit with him until he gets over it. I don't know why she did that. She must have known it wasn't going to win her any votes. Warfield, Harding, and Zabriskie were all so upset—their wives, too—that they decided not to come to the party after all. Enough was enough."

"What about Mike?"

"He's upstairs. We have our own wing, and our attorney advised us not to move out."

"Is your attorney here? I'd like to meet him if he is."

Tella twitched a smile. "No, she isn't here. Pam Calloway represents the family. Our side of it anyway."

"I bet she doesn't represent the three outside members."

"They're represented by Woodruff, Wallace, Manoukian and Lagomarsino." Her eyes were roaming past my shoulder again. "That firm also represented my father. But I don't like them. And I felt we should have someone without possible conflicts of interest on our side."

I winced. I didn't like being thought of in the same class with Woodruff, Wallace. Not that there was anything wrong with the firm, if you didn't mind bright, supposedly reputable men who lacked what in a simpler age would be called a fine ethical sensibility. And Sandra's husband, Don Echeverria, didn't. He was an associate in the firm.

"I don't blame you," I said.

"If you want to talk to Van Woodruff, he's by the fireplace."

I spotted Woodruff, a tall man with wings of gray hair, and turned slightly so that he wouldn't be likely to see me.

"Who represents your mother?"

"Norman Lagomarsino. He's there next to Van. Silly of her, isn't it?"

I could just see the top of a balding head.

"Doesn't sound smart. But if you think he'll sell her out, why hire me?" So much for my decision not to ask again. The question slipped out anyway.

"Insurance," Tella said brightly, with an emphasis that made me feel as if she was starting to wonder about my intelligence. "Besides, with both Woodruff and Lagomarsino collecting fees, why should they want to settle it in their lifetimes?"

"Okay." I sighed. "I'm still on the case."

"Good." She emptied the glass in one graceful motion. I could almost see champagne running down her long, white throat. "Call me when you have something to report. Make it soon."

Tella disappeared into the room as quickly as she had materialized. Beer in hand, I headed toward Gloria, to thank her and say good night.

"There you are, Freddie!" Gloria called over someone's midnight-blue shoulder. "What did you think of the show?"

"I thought it was amazing." Honesty was easier than I had thought it would be.

She reached out for the hand that wasn't holding the beer can and pulled me to her.

"Are you having a good time?"

That one was tougher.

"Actually, I was just coming over to say good-bye. I'm afraid I have to work tomorrow."

Made it.

"Do you have to rush away? I want to introduce you to Van Woodruff. He got a divorce last year, and he has to be the most eligible bachelor in Reno. Handsome, too." She nudged me and winked, between-us-girls.

"I appreciate the thought, but I met Van a couple of years ago, and we didn't hit it off." Close enough.

"Too bad." She frowned. "He was my first thought. You're not going to be like Tella, are you? She ridicules every man who shows the slightest interest in her. I've given up on her. If she wants to stay single, she can. It's her funeral."

"Well—" Hell. "I really don't want to disappoint you, Gloria. Maybe we can talk about it another time. Thank you for inviting me. It's time for me to be going."

"Yeah, yeah. I'm not giving up."

That's what I was afraid of.

I left the beer can on the Victorian hat rack, on the shelf

under the cloudy mirror. The fresh air was a relief. I crunched back down the gravel driveway and walked along the middle of the street to the Jeep.

As I drove home, I wondered if I should have said something to Tella about the snatch of conversation, the rumor about Warfield. But I suspected the possibility of a palace coup had already occurred to her.

I fed the cats and went to bed, then discovered I was too wired to sleep. I flicked through channels looking for a Western, but even Ted Turner—who can usually be counted on for one more rerun of Randolph Scott in *Buchanan Rides Alone*—failed me. TBS was saluting Annette Funicello and Frankie Avalon. I turned the set off and stared at the dark ceiling.

In truth, I understood the guy who wanted to sell his stock, even though he knew he would make more money by hanging on for the ride. If Tella won, Gloria lost. If Gloria won, Tella lost. If Warfield took over, they both lost. And who knew what would be best for the company. I certainly wasn't equipped to make that kind of judgment, and I wasn't even sure what the basis for making it would be. If Mike was really the major asset, then it ought to be his decision. The only thing I would absolutely bet the ranch on was that it wouldn't be.

I got up and did some stretching exercises to release the tension in my body. They helped a little, not enough. I went back to bed just in time to catch the classic Oedipal conflict of *The Brides of Dracula*. Fortunately, it bored me to sleep.

When the sunlight streaming in through the crack in the window blind woke me up, I was still ruminating, carried forward from a nightmare of competing seances to raise the ghost of Ted Scope. The one relief was that he never spoke to me. Never even tried.

I checked the computer for messages, hoping Rudy Stapp had picked up his and gotten back to me, but no luck there. For lack of anything better to do, I was early for lunch with Sandra, who breezed into Harrah's coffee shop at quarter after twelve.

"Now," she said as she slid into the booth. "What are you doing for which of the Scopes?"

"What do you know about them?" I countered.

"Unfortunately, probably nothing that will help you. I was as stunned as anyone else by Gloria's announcement last night." Sandra pushed the menu aside. Casino coffee shop menus have a comforting sameness, and Sandra always ordered a salad anyway. "I've had some contact with the family over the years because Daddy found Gloria unfailingly generous whenever the theater needed to be bailed out of a budget deficit. I would have described her as a woman who married well and knew it. She liked to indulge her eccentricities and considered herself lucky that she could pay for them. Is she paying for you?"

"No." I exhaled sharply. "Shit, Sandra. I don't know what to do. They all seem crazy to me."

A waitress, poised with pad in hand, interrupted the conversation. She turned first to Sandra, who was wearing an ivory dress with a peach jacket that made her look powerful and feminine at the same time. I truly admired her ability to consistently pull that off. She ordered, and I told the waitress to double the chicken salad and send the Keno runner.

"They all seem crazy because they are," Sandra said when the waitress had left. "I met Ted Scope at a couple of cast parties that Gloria dragged him to. He had the same weird eyes and pasty skin that his sons have, although his acne had cleared up. He didn't like coming to the theater.

While Gloria was in the center of the room demanding attention, Ted would be standing in a corner talking to a bookcase, unless he could find someone to talk business with. His negotiating skills were legendary, and I heard that in a conference room he could even be charming. As pudgy as both Ted and Gloria were, Tella must be borderline anorexic to stay so slender. I got to know her a little because she handled most of the press relations for Scope Chips. She's the most sensible one of them all—and the only attractive human being."

"You think she's a better choice to take over the company than Gloria?"

I must have let too much out on that one, because Sandra leaned forward and looked me in the eyes.

"Without question." She paused for emphasis. "I know you saved Gloria's life, and in some philosophies that makes you responsible for her. She's gutsy, too, and you'd like that about her. But Tella has both guts and vision. On top of that, she can handle her brothers. Gloria makes both of them worse."

"Both of them? I thought Mike was smart and sane."

Sandra shook her head.

"Mike's a genius, but he only seems sane next to Guy. They both need Tella."

The Keno runner flew by, collecting my ticket and my dollar without pausing.

"I wish this was making me feel better."

"Gambling doesn't make anyone feel better."

"Goddamn it, Sandra, let up on me. I meant the conversation."

"Sorry." She said it with a smile. "So if Tella hired you, what were you doing with Gloria?"

"I'll explain when I understand it. I don't suppose there's

any chance that Ted Scope's ghost will tell her to take *Oh, Nevada* to Broadway and forget about the company."

"I think Ted Scope's ghost will say whatever she wants it to—except when it talks to Guy—and I also think she hasn't fooled herself into believing this show has a shot at the big time."

"Do you think she might have gone to all the trouble of staging that show just as a prologue to the ghost story?"

Sandra nodded. "It occurred to me. Beyond that, there wasn't a lot of reason to do it. The Nevada bicentennial is almost seventy years away, and nobody else is going to be interested in Eilley Orrum and her crystal ball. At least not without a better score."

I watched the Keno numbers come up and pulled out a dollar to replay the ticket.

"What about Warfield?"

"What do you mean?"

"Is he a good guy or a bad guy?"

Sandra hesitated while the waitress served our salads.

"Warfield thinks the American economy revolves around the white male power structure as surely as the earth revolves around the sun. My guess is he's backing Tella against her mother because he thinks he can either control Tella—and through her, Mike—or get rid of her and convince Mike it was the best thing for the fortunes of all concerned. Does that make him a bad guy?"

"Maybe." I picked up my fork and realized I was hungry. "I need more information on that one."

"There's plenty available. He's a public man."

"But he belongs to a private club. A hunting club. With Harding and Zabriskie. And now Gloria."

Sandra washed down a bite of salad with iced tea, holding up her hand so I'd know she had something to say.

"He's not the kind of bad guy who would take a shot at Gloria, if that's where you're going. Although I'd love to be invited the first time Gloria crashes the party."

"Then you know about the club?"

"Only by rumor. If you can get me inside, I'll owe you, big time. Can you?"

This time I had to swallow before I answered. "Not unless Gloria has her own party there. If not Warfield, who might take a shot at Gloria?"

"The obvious choice is Guy, because he's the craziest and therefore the most likely to try something violent to scare her. If he even understands what's going on. Beyond that—" Sandra shrugged and took another bite.

"Yeah. Do the Woodruff, Wallace guys belong to the hunting club?"

She shook her head until her mouth was clear. "Not rich enough."

Neither one of us was getting enough to eat.

"Okay," I said. "Talk about your kid so I can eat and think about this and I don't have to pay attention."

"Don't invoke my glorious son's presence in vain. We'll eat in silence if you want to think."

That's what I love about having friends. I filled my mouth and gave the Keno runner the ticket to replay.

In fact, Sandra couldn't resist telling me the latest about her child. But she got even by asking about my mother.

"It's scary," I said, swallowing a too-big hunk of chicken. "Since all the little incision marks healed, she looks thirty-eight, tops. It's as if I don't have a mother. And don't jump on that."

"I wouldn't dream of it. And I have no advice."

At least I knew the problem was real.

Sandra had to dash back to work, and I didn't have to be

anywhere until it was time to look for Deke, to hear if he had come up with anything on Gloria.

Because I couldn't come up with an excuse not to, I spent a virtuous afternoon with the files. I had a warm feeling of accomplishment and a clean desk by eight o'clock, when it was time to walk to the Mother Lode.

The evening was just comfortably cool after a warm day. The sun had barely set, and the sky was pale indigo with pink-tinged clouds as I passed the old frame houses on Mill Street, catching an occasional TV voice blaring through an open window. I turned north on Virginia, crossed the Truckee River, and strolled into the amusement park, where flashing, rippling neon outshines the moon and the stars. I wondered what a fauve painter would have done with Virginia Street.

I crossed the air curtain into the Mother Lode, welcomed into the red haze of my home away from home by the scream of a slot machine announcing a big payoff. Coins crashed, lights blinked, and arms on either side continued to thunk coins without pause. The escalator carried me to the second-floor coffee shop.

"Tell me," I said, taking the stool next to Deke at the counter.

"Nothing to tell," he said.

"Couldn't you find anybody who knew Gloria?"

"Found a couple of people, but they both wanted to put her up for sainthood."

"Shit. That's no help." I waved at Diane, who brought me a beer.

"It's the best I could do. And it lets you off the hook with the daughter."

"Almost. I still have to check out New York."

"Maybe, maybe not."

"What do you mean?"

He regarded me through red-rimmed eyes before answering.

"Just that there was some subtext in the voices I talked to, emphasizing that the woman in question was above reproach."

"Some subtext? What the *hell* do you mean?"

"Just what I said. There's a text, a context, and a subtext. This was subtext."

I started peeling the label off my beer bottle.

"Thanks. I'll check New York."

"Or maybe you want to go to work for the mother. If you want my suggestion. And if you don't want to walk away from the whole thing, which I suspect you are already too involved to do."

"I suspect I am, too, Deke. I suspect I am, too."

Dinner wasn't exactly a thrill after that, but at least Deke didn't ask about my mother.

Walking home cheered me some, because the evening was still pleasant. And Butch and Sundance were glad to see me, if only because I hadn't fed them before I left.

I flicked through the channels and caught a reassuring glimpse of Randolph Scott in a cavalry uniform before I turned out the lights.

When I booted up the computer in the morning, I was cheered to discover that Ruby Stapp had finally answered my message. Until I read what he had to say.

"Larry Agnotti is a made wiseguy otherwise known as Larry the Lamb. I would strongly advise you not to pursue this inquiry unless someone has offered you a million dollars and a new identity on the other end."

Shit.

Chapter

4

CONSPIRACY THEORIES HAVE never interested me very much. When I lie awake at night staring at the ceiling, wondering whether a lone assassin shot JFK isn't what causes my synapses to arc. I don't believe that the entire state of Nevada is run by organized crime—or organized anything else. I think the large casinos are run pretty much as honestly or as dishonestly as most large corporations, and the Nevada Gaming Commission does a straightforward job of weeding out partners who keep bad company.

At the same time, having lived in Nevada all my life, I have a sense of the vast amounts of cash that flow through the casinos every day. I believe that some of it never finds its way to the ledgers. I also believe that some leaves the state cleaner than it arrives. My feeling that this goes on more in Las Vegas than in Reno is derived partly from chauvinism, partly from rumor, and partly from a practical awareness of how much bigger the action in Las Vegas since World War II has been.

So I didn't bother to ask how a Las Vegas PI would know something about a New York wiseguy.

I might have wondered how a mobster's about-to-be-ex-wife could work at a casino, but Tella had said that her

mother had worked under the name Gloria Fry. The Mother
Lode had been owned by Charlie Barrington in those days,
and I could imagine that Charlie would have been more than
willing to rack up some brownie points by doing somebody
a quiet favor, especially since the name Fry wouldn't have
raised any eyebrows.

I sat there in my cracked leather chair behind my garage
sale desk trying to figure out what the hell I should do with
the information.

Butch jumped up on my lap and blocked the screen with
his waving gray tail, but it didn't help. I still knew what it
said. I pushed his rear end, trying to get him to sit so that I
could see the message and think at the same time, but he
squawked in protest and hopped onto the desk, scattering
the papers that I had sorted the day before and hadn't gotten
around to filing yet.

I knew I had to call Tella. She was my client—I had, after
all, deposited the check and then made the inquiries on her
behalf. I was also prepared to write her a check for the part
of the retainer I hadn't earned—and didn't plan to, because
I was taking Rudy's advice. I had had enough reservations
about this case to begin with, and the thought that I might be
kicking the shins of organized crime had tilted the balance.

I hoped that calling Tella would make the whole situation
quietly go away. Maybe Gloria wouldn't want the world to
know that her first husband was a member of the mob. Even
in Reno, that wouldn't go down very well. Maybe Tella
would decide she couldn't fling mud at Gloria without
splattering her white suit. Maybe they could negotiate their
differences. Hope struggled to flow through constricted
veins into my heart.

I picked up the phone and punched Tella's number. I had

thought it was a direct line, but I still had to get past a gatekeeper.

"We need to meet," I told her when she picked up.

"Mondays are terribly hectic," she replied. "You'll either have to tell me over the phone or wait until tomorrow."

"No. I'm giving you my one and only report and a refund. I can't do it over the phone and I won't wait until tomorrow."

The tone convinced her.

"Stop by my office at three. I'll fit you in."

I hung up and pushed Butch off the desk so I could write the check. I had to fight a moment of depression as I contemplated what I could have done with the money.

The building that housed Scope Chips was on Kietzke Lane, just north of the intersection with Virginia Street. I gave myself fifteen minutes to drive there, knowing I'd be early. The high, clear June sky with its wisps of white clouds called to me. As I passed Plumb Lane, I had to fight an impulse to head for the airport and take off in the Cherokee. I didn't do it because I don't try to fly away from my problems. They're always still there when I come back to earth.

The entrance to the grounds was almost obscured by the hedges that ran smack into the pavement. Like the house, the plant had no sidewalks. I turned right and stopped immediately at a guardhouse. SCOPE CHIPS was printed on a small sign below the window, the only indication that I was in the right place. Someone had decided not to advertise the firm's presence.

The guard checked my name on a list and then asked for picture identification before raising the crossarm. I pulled into a large parking lot in front of one of those flat, gray, one-story structures that make light industrial blocks all look alike and eased into a space next to a teal-blue BMW with a license plate that read CHIPS2.

Inside the glass front door was a narrow reception area with a white leather couch and chair and a low coffee table covered with magazines. The kind of sliding window usually found in dentists' offices opened to reveal a woman in her mid-twenties with mahogany skin and gold hoop earrings who compared name, face, and ID one more time before she pressed a buzzer that opened a solid door.

"Diagonally through the open area to the closed door in the far corner," she said. I recognized the lilt in her voice from the telephone call. "Miss Scope said to send you right in."

I walked through the door into the so-called open area. It wasn't exactly empty space. It was a room that must have taken up half the building, filled with carefully arranged workstations. Clusters of three or four desks allowed people to exchange information without moving from their computer terminals. There were maybe twenty men and women, none over forty, and none of them did more than glance at me as I tried to negotiate a diagonal.

The other half of the building was walled off, with two closed doors. The one with a window led to the gatekeeper's cubicle. I'd have to ask about the second. Besides the door at the end of the diagonal that marked Tella's office, there were two others on the far wall. At least one wall of the open area had to double as a building wall, but none of them had windows. No views of the parking lot to distract anyone from work.

Before I could knock on the blank door at the far end of the room, it swung open. Tella was sitting behind a desk in a room much smaller than I had expected. The windows behind her were almost overgrown with shrubbery, but the view beyond them was only more of the parking lot.

"What opened the door?" I asked.

"An electronic sensor," she answered. She swiveled away from a computer screen and faced me, this time wearing a loose, pale green jacket over a white silk blouse. I was impressed again by her marble beauty and her self-possession. "It's the best of both worlds—I can have an open-door policy without actually leaving the door open. That allows me to work undisturbed unless someone wants to see me."

"I'd be surprised if you got many drop-ins. Why all the security?"

"Symbolism, really." She smiled, looking really young for the first time. "We don't really worry about industrial espionage. The assets of the company walk out the front door and drive home every night, but we want them to remember how valuable they are. Besides, it impresses the Pentagon types."

"I'm sure it does. But there have to be other assets as well—like whatever is behind the wall."

"We do have a mainframe computer. Two in tandem, in case one goes down. My father's idea of security. Most of the work is done on linked microprocessors now. Have a seat."

She gestured toward one of two chairs in front of the desk. The seats and backs were upholstered with a nubby slate, black, and white plaid. The arms were smooth, dark wood. They were attractive, but not so comfortable that a visitor would be inclined to stay too long. The rest of the office was utilitarian. No pictures, no plants, no signs of a home-away-from-home. This was a work space, nothing more.

I had the refund check in my pocket. I pulled it out and placed it on the desk in front of her, on a clear spot next to the keyboard. She didn't even glance at it. Her smile barely tightened as she waited.

"According to a reliable source, Gloria's first husband, Larry Agnotti, is connected with organized crime. A 'made wiseguy' was the phrase used. If you plan to use that information, you might want to do it carefully."

Tella slapped the desk in glee.

"I told you there was something to find. Do you think that's all? Is that why you're quitting?"

"Oh, God, Tella." I shut my eyes, hoping that an inspiration would come to me. None did, and I had to continue anyway. "My informant says that Gloria's days at the casino were clean. I don't know what kind of life she lived before she moved to Reno—besides marrying Larry Agnotti and then deciding to divorce him—but I have been advised by two people whose judgment I respect that I shouldn't try to find out, because Larry Agnotti might not like it."

That wasn't exactly what Deke had advised, but it was close enough.

"I'm not on any kind of crusade here," I continued, opening my eyes to look at her. "Scope Chips isn't worth nosing around the mob for."

"It is to me." Tella's wide blue eyes stared straight into mine. "Do you watch a lot of television?"

"What? Some—I don't know what you'd consider a lot. Why?"

"I just thought that worrying about the mob was something that happened on television. I don't care who Larry Agnotti is. This is my company, and I'm not giving it up for anyone."

I decided that struggling with her naïveté wasn't part of my job.

"Then discuss this with your mother," I said, staring right back. "I'll even sit down with the two of you, if you think that will help."

That slipped out, and I would have bitten my tongue off to take it back. I didn't want to act as mediator, and in truth, I didn't think I'd be very good at it. I thought about reminding her that this shouldn't be just her decision, that a lot of other people were involved in the company, too, but I didn't think she'd like it.

"Maybe." She rocked the swivel chair as she thought about what I'd said. Then she leaned forward, picked up the check, and tore it in half. I winced at how easily she did it. "The money was a retainer, and you don't owe it back. Besides, you may earn it yet."

I was afraid of that.

"Two days ago someone took a shot at your mother," I reminded her. "That wasn't something from a television show."

"Do you think it was him? Her ex-husband?"

"No. I don't. I think it was someone trying to scare her. And finding out who it was is police business, not mine. But if I were you, I'd be concerned."

Tella frowned. "The police don't have a clue. I talked to the detective, Matthews. All he knows is that the dust in the bell tower had been disturbed. He thinks it may have been some kind of prank, since no one was hurt. I think you're right—someone was trying to scare her. And didn't. He didn't scare me, either."

I already knew that.

"He?" I asked.

"Whoever. The lack of subtlety is the mark of a male

mind." She looked at me as if she hoped I'd share the joke. I didn't.

"And your tales about the mob don't scare me, either," she added.

I sighed. "Call me if you need me."

The sensor opened the door as I stepped toward it.

"I will," she said cheerfully.

I retraced my steps through the maze of desks and rapped on the gatekeeper's window. She buzzed me out. No automatic exit to the outer sanctum.

The afternoon was still gorgeous, the hills to the west were a crisp, shiny brown, like fresh donuts, and I felt another tug as I retraced the drive along Kietzke, passing within a few blocks of the airport.

As I turned the corner off Mill Street, I wished I had stopped at the airport. My mother's wine-colored Oldsmobile was parked in front of my house, and she was standing at the driver's door, just about to get back in. If I had dawdled, I could have missed her.

She closed the door and waved when she spotted me.

I pulled the Jeep into the driveway and met her at the steps to the house.

"I was in town doing some shopping, and I just stopped by to see if you were here. What do you think of my new boots?"

She did a little twirl to show them off. They were white, with stiletto heels and toes that tapered unnaturally, decorated with silver studs and white fringe. I thought they were disgusting—the American equivalent of Chinese foot bindings—but she was smiling, so I searched for something kind.

"They look cheerful," I said, not looking her in the eye. "And they match your jumpsuit."

The jumpsuit was light blue denim with more silver studs. "That's what I thought." Her smile bloomed.

"Do you want to come in?"

I asked to be polite, hoping she'd say no. I was still having trouble dealing with her surgically enhanced face, even though the man who did it could have been a sculptor, the lines were so aesthetically perfect.

In truth, I've always had trouble dealing with my mother, who is eight inches shorter than I am, even in her spike heels, and weighs probably fifty pounds less than I do. I'm not overweight, but I have large bones and a bit of muscle on them. Ramona has the sleek frame of a Siamese cat.

My mother had always been beautiful, and had never shown the years. The copper curls had seemed right on her the first time I saw them, never a cover-up for gray. The smooth chin and round eyes, the same hazel that mine are, were those of a woman who had yet to confront middle age. The thought occurred to me that Ramona's spirit was better reflected by her new face. I would learn—I was determined to learn—to accept this woman who looked young enough to be my sister. Even if the only resemblance was the color of our eyes.

"I just have a minute," she said. "I told Al I'd be home in time for dinner."

I hoped the relief didn't show in my face. Ramona and Al, my stepfather, lived at Lake Tahoe, which was just about the right distance. We could get together if we had to, but the drive was an excuse to miss anything short of Christmas.

"Okay. Another time."

A yowl from the railing signaled that Sundance had realized she was here. Sometimes I've thought he adored her to spite me, because Butch was the dominant one of the two toms, and throwing himself at Ramona got attention.

"Hello, sweetheart," Ramona said, reaching out to scratch his furry orange back. He stretched, arching his tail. "I have to leave, baby, but I'll see you soon." She said that to Sundance, not to me. Then she turned back to me and added, "You don't have to check in with me, you know that. You're an adult, and even though I can't say I don't worry about you anymore, because I do, I respect your right to lead your own life."

"I'm sorry," I broke in. "I should have called you over the Gloria Scope thing."

"Whether you should have called isn't the issue. I just want you to remember that I care. I'd also appreciate it if you would remember Al's position and warn us when you're going to be in the papers."

"Damn. You're right, Ramona, I didn't think of Al. I also didn't think that a mention of me in connection with Gloria Scope would have any effect whatsoever on a state assemblyman representing Tahoe."

The smooth skin on her face couldn't give enough to frown.

"I didn't stop by to upset you. I think you did a wonderful job protecting the Scope woman, and I hope you feel better now about being a bodyguard. And if you want to come up to the lake sometime this summer, you'd be welcome, you know that."

"I know. Thanks for asking."

I couldn't tell her I wasn't Gloria's bodyguard. It would just get us into a whole new conversation that I wasn't up for.

She held up her hand, in a sort of wave, then started down the steps.

"Ramona? You look like a movie star."

She turned, glowing.

"Do you think so?"

"I think so." And I wasn't sure it was a compliment, but I knew she would think it was. I watched her drive away.

The phone was ringing as I unlocked the front door and let myself into the office. I grabbed it right before the machine answered.

"Freddie, honey, what have you done?" Gloria asked. I shriveled at the sound of her voice. "You told Tella about Larry? Why?"

"She hired me. She must have told you that. I had a contract with her—I had to let her know what I found out."

The words sounded pathetic.

"Why couldn't you have told me first?"

"Because it would have been unethical. I'm sorry—I really am. The whole thing got a lot more complicated than I thought it was going to be."

"Yeah, yeah. I understand. I'm not happy, but I understand. And if you hadn't told her, she would have hired somebody else who would have told her."

"I thought of that, too." But it didn't help me feel any better.

"Okay. Tella said you offered to mediate, just the three of us, no attorneys. I don't think it'll help, but I think it's a good thing to try. How about nine o'clock tonight? Can you be here?"

I shifted in my chair, wishing for a way to get out of saying yes.

"I can be there," I said.

After Gloria hung up, I turned on the computer, but there were no new messages. I pulled up Tetris. I had just discovered it and was instantly addicted to watching the blocks fall, even though I hadn't expected the game to interest me.

I managed to amuse myself mindlessly until it was time to feed the cats and leave for the castle.

This time there were no cars on the street, none in the gravel driveway, and no valet parkers to avoid. I left the Jeep on the far side of the front turret, in the shadow of a pine tree. Spotlights caused patches of brightness on the grounds, but the trees reclaimed the dark wherever they could.

Gloria met me at the door, before I could bang the lion's head. She was wearing a lavender Moroccan-inspired gown with some kind of floor-length vest falling from her shoulders, the same lavender striped with purple. I suspected some saleswoman had told her vertical stripes were slimming.

"We can sit in the library," she said. "I buzzed Tella on the intercom when I saw your car."

She led me past the Victorian hat rack, past the door to the room where the party had been, to an atrium covered with an Oriental carpet. Stairs swept up the left side, and a balcony ran around the second floor. On the far wall a larger-than-life saint was being martyred, perfectly illuminated by track lighting. We skipped the stairs and took the hall on the right. The library was the last door before the changing shape of the wall signaled the west turret.

The walls were lined with shelves, neatly packed with books. A low sofa and two chairs, in matching forest-green velvet, faced a glowing gas-log fireplace with brass andirons. This was an interior decorator's idea of a library, not a place where I could imagine anyone reading or studying. And it seemed particularly incongruous in a house bought with high-tech money. Especially when the original owner was a gambler with a street education.

But that might make it neutral territory for Gloria and Tella, and a good place for a meeting.

"There's coffee and brandy on the tray," Gloria said. "But if you want something else, I'll get it."

"Coffee will be fine." I didn't really want it, but brandy gives me headaches. And I couldn't think of anything I did want, except to get this over with.

The tray and coffee urn were silver, the kind of old silver that glows in the firelight. The tray also held three fragile cups and saucers, a decanter of brandy, and three snifters. Gloria poured coffee for me, brandy for herself, then leaned back in the chair, swirling the brandy in the glass as if it were something she did often.

I sat on the couch, awkwardly, without enough room for my legs. I struggled to come up with something to say, other than that I was sorry I got involved in this. But Tella was in the room before I came up with anything.

As she dropped into the chair facing her mother, I was jolted by her appearance. She was wearing jeans and a white shirt, cut Western style. Her hair was brushed back from her face, which was clean of makeup. She might have been a college student, just a year or two old for her class. The statement—that she was like me, really—was unnerving. And too theatrical to be convincing.

"Where do we start?" she asked.

"I start," Gloria answered. She took a moment, still swirling the brandy. When she spoke, her voice was low and calm. "Ted created the business. His brains, his guts. Without Ted there would have been no Scope Chips. You and Mike and Guy wouldn't have the education, the advantages—this house—everything—if it hadn't been for Ted. So everything was his to dispose of however he wanted. And he wanted to give it to me." Tella opened her mouth, but Gloria held up a hand to stop her. "I know that's tough for you to accept. I'm not saying he didn't appreciate your contribution. He did. He thought the world of the three of you. In ten years he might have made different decisions, might have rewritten his will and revised the trust. But speculating about that isn't going to do us any good right now. The fact is, he left everything in the trust and asked me to take care of it. So that's what I'm going to do. I'll do it with you if you want to work with me. Otherwise I'll do it without you."

"You want us to work for you, not work with you. You don't know how to work with people." Tella's voice was as low and as calm as her mother's. "Daddy was sick, and he wasn't thinking about what was best for the business. He didn't think the world of us, not ever. He was only thinking about himself, about how great he was. And there was a time when he was great, but it was years ago." She watched Gloria, but Gloria's face didn't quiver. "Putting everything in a trust with you in charge was as close as he could get to taking it with him. A living memorial. No change. And that alone would be bad enough in an industry that has to reinvent itself every six months. Worse is the position it puts Mike in—and it's Mike's brain that counted before, more than Daddy was willing to admit, and counts even more now. Does he stay as a hired hand in his own house? Or does he walk away and start his own company? We could do that, you know—leave you with a shell."

Gloria shook her head. "You have the guts for that, Mike doesn't. He couldn't stand the uncertainty. You think if you force Mike to choose between the cozy spot he's been working in since he was a teenager, with me making decisions instead of his father, and some new, unknown life with you in charge, he'll go with you. When push comes to shove, he might not."

"He'd go with me." Tella was unmoved. "But for push to come to shove, you'd have to win both the court battle and the proxy fight."

I felt as if I were watching a slow, calculated tennis match as I turned from one to the other. But that was fine. I could handle observing.

"I'll chance it," Gloria said. "I have the guts, too."

"Your odds of winning drop considerably once we expose your former marriage to the mob," Tella responded.

"That was a long time ago. I was younger then than you are now. Who says I knew what Larry did? Who can even prove he did it then? I'm not responsible for Larry. I admire you, baby—I have from the day when you were four years old and you announced to Ted that he didn't have to read you a bedtime story because you could read it yourself. And you read *Paddington Bear* to him, without a mistake, just the way he read it to you the night before. He called me in to hear, and you did it again. We thought maybe you had some weird kind of memory, so the next day Ted bought a copy of *The Wonderful Wizard of Oz*, and damned if you didn't open the cover and start reading it." Gloria set her snifter down on the coffee table and leaned forward. "But as brave and smart as you are, you can't always have what you want when you want it. If you want to run the company, you have to hang in. You have to wait until I'm dead."

Tella turned to me with a smile.

"You see where we are, Freddie," she said.

My coffee was cold, and I hadn't wanted it to begin with. I put it down next to Gloria's snifter.

"Yeah, I see where we are." I looked from one to the other. "I wish I could help you, but I don't even know how to begin. I just don't have the skills for this. I don't know what else to tell you."

I stood up and headed for the door.

"Drive carefully," Gloria called.

I walked down the hall, past the martyred saint and the Victorian hat rack, and out the door. My Jeep was still in its shadow.

The drive home seemed long and exhausting, even though it was just a few miles. Something about that meeting had sucked all the energy out of me. Even though it wasn't late, all I wanted to do was crawl into bed with the cats. But when I tried, they chose that moment to fight over who got the extra pillow and who took the foot of the bed, before jumping off the mattress in different directions.

Sleep seemed even more elusive than love, but I caught it sometime close to dawn.

I woke up rested and cheerful. I had dreamed that the situation was resolved, and I could go on with my life. The dream felt like good advice.

The cozy feeling lasted until afternoon, when the phone rang.

"Gloria Scope was murdered last night," Sandra said. "They've arrested her son."

Chapter 5

I HATED ADMITTING it, even to myself. And in fact I only admitted it to myself. But the emotion washing over me when I heard about Gloria Scope's murder was relief, relief that I hadn't agreed to be her bodyguard. I had no faith that I could have prevented her murder, and I simply couldn't have handled the kind of substantive failure that losing a client—terminally losing a client—represented. I would have closed my business and looked for another line of work.

Then I felt guilty about the relief.

Only after that could I feel diminished by her death.

According to the police reporter who was Sandra's source, Gloria had been clubbed with a blunt object and dumped in the swimming pool. The heavy solar cell cover, which clung to the surface of the water, had held her under. The coroner would have to determine whether the blow or the water killed her. The gardener had discovered the body in the morning.

There aren't a lot of swimming pools in Reno, because the season for using them is fairly short. Sometimes it snows as late as Easter. Dying in your own swimming pool was a hazard reserved for the wealthy.

A lousy way for Gloria to end.

Sandra wasn't certain just why Guy—it was, of course, the crazy one, not the smart one—had been arrested. The police had kept it fairly quiet. Her buddy had heard Guy was claiming something about extraterrestrial involvement. Nobody expected him to stand trial.

A neat way to wrap it up.

I knew I should get in touch with Tella, express sympathy, offer to work off somehow the rest of the money she had paid me. But I couldn't help thinking how convenient this was for her. And I couldn't help wondering what earthly force—UFOs be damned—had influenced Guy to hit his mother over the head.

The murder was on the local news that evening and all over the *Herald* the next morning. Unfortunately, I had an appointment with the dentist that afternoon, and Tyler Urrutia, the hygienist, was hoping I knew something not in the papers. She had decided the first time she cleaned my teeth that I had the inside track on all Reno crime, and I hadn't been able to dissuade her in five years.

Tyler had wide dark eyes and long dark hair, and she was the cousin of somebody I used to have a crush on. I didn't hold that against her. What I held against her was that she asked me questions and poked my gums with sharp instruments at the same time. I felt like Dustin Hoffman in *Marathon Man*.

I would have gotten away with shrugs and grunts, except that Dr. Berman came in while she was chattering, having just finished with the flossing, and I found myself asking him a question. About pulling healthy teeth, and whether he would do it.

"I wouldn't do it," he said as he checked my chart. As charts go, it was a long one. He had been my dentist since

I was twelve. I was suddenly conscious of his white hair and the lines in his hands, and I wondered how old he was. I didn't know what I would do when he retired. Aside from my mother, Dr. Berman was the only lasting relationship in my life. Even though, or maybe because, I only saw him twice a year. "But I don't pull anyone's teeth anymore. I don't like to do it, so I send patients to an oral surgeon."

He closed the folder and looked at me, through pale blue eyes behind heavy glasses. "We used to talk about situations like that in dental school. Some guys said they wouldn't pull healthy teeth. Others said they would if it was a cash transaction and the patient knew the risks. Bobby Fischer, the chess champ, had all his teeth pulled, and so did the wacko hippie who assassinated that Stanford professor, Loewenstein, fifteen or twenty years ago. Both of them claimed UFOs—and I think the FBI and CIA, too—were interfering with their lives through their fillings. So some dentists still pull teeth. Are you ready for new X rays? The ones we have are three years old, and you talked your way out of it last time you were in."

"The photographic plates make me gag," I said. "And I still have the same mouth."

"I worry about those wisdom teeth. I'd feel better with a new X ray."

His brow creased from worry about my wisdom teeth.

"Did Guy Scope have all his teeth pulled?" Tyler asked. "Is that why you want to know about it?"

"You'll have to ask his dentist," I replied, with all the innocence I could muster.

"You can tell me, Freddie, and I promise I won't pass it on. Everybody says he's crazy anyway." She squirmed with eagerness, and I knew the conversation would be repeated to the next victim in her chair.

"I'd be surprised if he had." Dr. Berman saved me from answering. "He's so young, he couldn't have had many fillings to start with. Most kids his age had their adult teeth treated with fluoride and sealers as soon as they came in. You're a few years older, and look how well your teeth have done—except for those wisdom teeth. The top ones are both at bad angles, and they aren't any good for chewing. They're just going to slice up the insides of your cheeks if you don't have them out. We could send the new X rays to the oral surgeon for you."

"Is there any reason why someone his age would have false teeth?" I asked, determined to distract him.

"Badly neglected caries. Gum disease. Cancer. Of course there are reasons. But you'd have to talk to his dentist." The smile said he saw right through me.

Dr. Berman got the X rays, and I bargained to save my wisdom teeth for another six months. Not that I thought he was wrong. They probably weren't doing me any good. But they weren't bothering me, either.

I walked out of the Arlington Medical Building into the bright June sunshine wishing I didn't feel there were so many unanswered questions surrounding Gloria Scope's death. The building was a square, two-story brick structure, out of place in a residential neighborhood, but probably older than zoning laws prohibiting it.

By the time I had followed the sidewalk down California to Virginia Street, I had fallen into an easy pace, almost enjoying the afternoon. The trees were green, the breeze ruffling the leaves was gentle, the roses were blooming in front yards along the way, the sky was cloudless. And the murder was none of my business.

The blinking light on the telephone answering machine

greeted me as I entered my office. I hit the Playback button and crossed my fingers, hoping for a new client.

What I got was a message from the dead.

"This is a little awkward," a man's voice began. "My name is Curtis Breckinridge. Gloria Scope called me Monday, asking if I could come for dinner one night soon. She said she wanted me to meet someone—you, actually."

He paused so long that the machine hung up on him. But he called back.

"Curtis Breckinridge again. I'd still like to meet you. And I think it might be a nice gesture to Gloria if we at least had a drink."

He left two phone numbers, work and home. The next message was about a job, but I had to play it back three times before I could concentrate on it. The last message was from Tella.

I returned Tella's call first. Fortunately, I missed her.

Next I called about the job, which was from a collection agency that hired me on a contract basis when the regular crew was overloaded. I hated hassling people who had financial troubles, but if I didn't, somebody else would, and accepting the work kept me from financial troubles of my own.

That left the call from the guy.

Did I want a blind date with a friend of Gloria's? Oddly, if she had been alive, it would have been easier to say no.

I checked the time, and the office number was the one to use. I called him back.

He answered on the first ring. He had a pleasant voice, not deep, and it lifted even more when I told him who it was.

"Great," he said. "I wasn't sure you'd call."

"I liked Gloria," I replied. "And a memorial drink sounded like a good idea."

"I liked her, too. Although I didn't know her very well—I met her at the reception when the computer lab opened."

"The university computer lab?"

"Yes. I'm a professor in the business school."

"Oh."

That put me off a little. I don't think much of business as an academic discipline. I run my own business, and it isn't that hard to learn. But I figured I was still stuck for a drink. Besides, maybe he taught computer programming. That was at least useful for helping students get a job.

"When is a good time to get together?" he asked.

"Tonight? Six o'clock?" Might as well get it over with.

"Great," he said again. "Where? I've only been in Reno since last September, and I don't know it very well, so you'll have to pick the place."

I rarely went anywhere but the Mother Lode, and I didn't want to meet him there. Too likely to run into Deke, and then I'd have to explain. I couldn't think of a quiet place except a restaurant or hotel bar, and I didn't want him to think I was angling for dinner. I picked a hotel within walking distance.

"The corner bar of the Sierra Madre," I said. "The one overlooking the river. How will I know you?"

"I'm tall, and what hair I have is dark. I'm wearing jeans and a sport coat. You?"

"I'm tall, too. A lot of hair, blond. Jeans and a denim jacket."

We figured we could spot each other.

At quarter to six the sun was still above the mountains, and it felt too early for a drink. I turned the computer off—you know you've been playing too much Scrabble when you beat the computer 426 to 211—and did a cursory check in the bathroom mirror. My teeth gleamed, and the rest of me was passable.

I walked the few blocks down Mill and turned right on Virginia, my usual route, but this time I crossed the street just short of the Truckee River instead of staying on the Mother Lode side. The water had a summer sparkle.

The bar had a street entrance, so I didn't have to cross the hotel lobby. I was momentarily blinded by the dim lighting, an artificial recreation of candlepower. The windows were tinted, subduing the river glow.

When I could see again, I checked the room. Three people were at the bar, and one man was alone at a table. He stood as my eyes got to him. I moved the few steps to the table, and he held out his hand.

"Curtis Breckinridge," he said.

"Freddie O'Neal," I answered.

He had a firm handshake. And he was a good height. We were eye to eye. His face went with his voice, pleasant and smooth, with features that didn't call attention to themselves. He had more hair than I expected, although male pattern baldness had obviously struck some years earlier. The sport jacket was a light tweed, and it covered an open-necked blue work shirt with a button-down collar. Button-down collars on work shirts have always puzzled me. Who would wear a work shirt with a tie? And what's the point of a button-down collar without a tie?

"You are tall," Curtis said. "I'm not used to meeting women as tall as I am."

He released my hand and we sat, awkwardly, having to pay attention, the way people suddenly forget how to sit when they meet a blind date.

"Yeah, I know."

"Gloria told me you saved her life. She said you're a private investigator."

"I didn't save it for very long."

Curtis frowned, afraid he'd made a mistake. The cocktail waitress rescued us. I ordered a draft beer.

"What wines do you pour by the glass?" Curtis asked.

"Inglenook, red or white," the waitress answered, bored by the question.

"I'll have mineral water, then, with a twist," he said.

"It'll have to be club soda," she told him.

He nodded, disappointed.

"We don't have to stay here," I said.

"No, no, it's fine, really it is." He sounded as if he wanted desperately to do the right thing.

The waitress had paused long enough to make sure we were going to stay. She turned away without a word.

"Do you teach programming?" I asked, hoping he'd say yes.

"Uh, no. I'm in leadership studies."

"What?"

"Leadership studies." His high forehead creased with enthusiasm. "I study leaders. In dynamic and turbulent environments, such as the one facing modern corporations, leadership makes the difference between success and failure."

"Really? I would have thought it was technology." I spoke before I thought, and he smiled, pleased that I seemed interested.

"Most people think that," he said earnestly, brow still creased, "and of course it's true in some situations. But most businesses don't depend on technology for profitability. They depend on people, and people depend on leaders."

"For what?"

The question startled him, but he answered gamely.

"Leaders shape and communicate the guiding vision of the organization and empower their employees to carry it out. The idea is to align personal and corporate goals, so both can be met. Everybody wins."

I remember Sandra saying that Tella had vision and guts. Whatever Curtis was talking about, the vocabulary was seeping into the culture.

"I would have thought what most people want from the organizations they work for is to be let alone while they do their jobs."

I really wanted to change the subject before I said something that offended him, but the response came out anyway.

"You would think that," Curtis answered, not in the least bothered. "You're an entrepreneur, and entrepreneurs are a special group."

"I'm self-employed," I corrected. "Ted Scope was an entrepreneur."

"The difference is size of operation, not style," he said, cheerfully ignoring the waitress as she set the drinks in front of us. "In support of that, let me see if I can tell you a few things about yourself, even though we've just met."

I was a little wary of the game, but I nodded.

"You've already told me you don't want to work for somebody else, that you want to do your job without supervision," he continued. "You're probably an only child. If you have any siblings, they're considerably younger. Your father was in business for himself."

I tried to control my wince on that one. I must have succeeded, because he kept going.

"You have a strong need for achievement, and you believe you control your own destiny. You can even be compulsive about taking responsibility for yourself, not depending on others. So you concentrate on work more than you do on relationships. You have a high tolerance for ambiguity—you neither need nor expect one day to be much like the next—and you have a high tolerance for risk, as long as you think the odds favor you."

He paused, smiling triumphantly, but I wasn't ready to leap in.

"I might add," he added, "that you're intelligent, educated, and competitive."

"Do you tell fortunes at the carnival on your days off?" I asked.

"No." He looked down, and I think he blushed. It was hard to tell in the glow of the tiny lamp on our table. "Social sciences aren't always exact, but they're a little more certain than tarot cards. I just described the profile of successful women entrepreneurs. There haven't been many studies done, and they're all first generation, but the results have been consistently replicated. We're seeing a second generation of women managers now, and they're significantly different from their predecessors. The same will probably be true with women entrepreneurs."

"What about leadership professors? Has anybody studied them?"

"No, I don't think so." He chuckled, nervously. "Either we do the studying, and never think to look at ourselves, or nobody else thinks we're very interesting. Or both. I know of one study on job satisfaction that included university professors as a group—we like our jobs a lot."

"I'm not letting you off that easily. Give me a profile of leadership professors."

"Well—it will have to be anecdotal, not scientific."

"Does anecdotal mean you'll be making it up as you go along?"

"Something like that. I can come up with a description based on a few colleagues and myself, but the database is limited, and my remarks speculative."

I leaned forward onto my elbows.

"Just do it," I said.

"I'd call us the humanists of the business school." His features became animated. He obviously liked his own phrase. "Even more so than the ethicists, who tend to get bogged down in cultural relativity. We're the ones arguing for human dignity, for the worth of the individual. We're the ones who insist that maximizing shareholder profits is not the only goal of the corporation."

"On top of that, you're intelligent, educated, and competitive," I said.

"Educated by definition, I suppose, and we like to think we're intelligent. I'd have to think about competitive, but you're probably right."

He beamed at me, and I found myself starting to like him, even if he did have an idiotic job.

"What, actually, do you teach?" I asked. "What would I learn if I took a course in leadership?"

"I don't know."

He said it so innocently that my jaw dropped.

"Really," he continued. "Women are socialized to be better leaders than men are. They're interested in power not for its own sake, but because there's an agenda to accomplish. So they tend to be more inclusive, more inclined to hire people to shore up their own weaknesses, less insistent on hogging credit. Much of what I do in my class is encourage the male students to emulate Gandhi rather than

Patton and tell the women students to go for it and not let the boys stand in their way."

"Do they listen to you?"

"Some do, some don't, like anything else."

"Did you meet Tella Scope?"

"What? Who? Oh—Gloria's daughter." Curtis's face went from puzzlement to recognition. The transition probably seemed abrupt to him, but I'd been thinking about her as he talked about psychological profiles. "That's such an embarrassing name. I'd expect her to change it now that both her parents are gone. Yes, I met her at the reception, the same night I met her mother."

"What do you think of her?"

"First I have to explain that Gloria tried to push us together, and Tella would have none of it."

I nodded. I had expected that, and I was glad he hadn't tried to hide it.

"Beyond that," he said, smiling as if relieved that I hadn't commented, "I think she's got the right stuff to run the company. I told her mother that, but Gloria just patted me on the head, and she could barely reach my head."

"Vision and guts," I said, echoing Sandra's comment.

"Exactly. Both of them have that. Or had. It's just that Gloria's vision seemed to be rooted in what Ted wanted, which may not be the best way for the company to go. She offered to hire me as a consultant, but I didn't think I was the right choice for the job."

"Why not?"

"Because I thought she should just turn everything over to her daughter." The implication was that I should have figured it out already. His raised eyebrows went halfway to his receding hairline.

"You'll never get rich that way, Curtis."

"I know." He sighed and looked at the table, registering that I had finished my beer. "Do you want another? Or would you like to go somewhere for dinner?"

"I am getting hungry," I admitted. I couldn't plead another engagement. Lying to this guy would be a mortal sin. "But I don't know anyplace that pours vintage wine by the glass."

"The hotel dining room probably has a respectable half bottle on the wine list. If you won't join me in something a little better."

I shook my head. "I don't understand the whole wine thing."

"Then order what you want." He pulled out his wallet. I reached for mine, but he grabbed my wrist. "I asked you. When you ask me, you can pay."

I had to laugh, which was clearly what he wanted.

"A deal," I said.

He settled with the waitress, and we left the bar. We were immediately in the casino area, the brightness and the loudness contrasting sharply with the coziness of the lounge. We meandered through rows of clanking slot machines to the restaurant. Curtis bobbed a little as he moved, as if he were used to walking with short people.

The restaurant was quiet, but everything in it—the leather banquettes, the menu covers, the pattern on the wallpaper—was casino red, except the maître d's suit and tie, which were black. Not that the place was formal. Most people were in business suits, although Curtis and I weren't the only ones in jeans.

When I saw the prices, I hoped he would let me split the bill. I didn't want this to be an expensive evening for him.

Dinner turned out to be okay. Not so much the food—I ordered prime rib, but Curtis made the mistake of ordering trout. If I'd known him a little better, I would have warned him that trout is terrific when it's caught in the morning and pan fried for breakfast, but it loses flavor almost immediately. He ate most of it, though, and he didn't complain.

The conversation was better. Curtis's undergraduate degree was in political science, and he was interested in the politics of crime and punishment. We pretty much agreed that the need to create jobs was greater than the need to build more prisons. I pointed out that the new state prison in Lovelock was going to be filled with guys who were still in grammar school when the plans were drawn.

"Just how will leadership studies do something to change that?" I asked.

"I'm not arguing that leadership studies will solve all the problems of society," he said. "On the other hand, I think we'd have a more civilized world if everybody believed that he or she had a shot at making a vision come true. And I try to give students a few tools that will help them do that."

I still wasn't convinced his work was useful, but I was a little less ready to put it down by the time we got to dessert.

Over coffee, we were back to Gloria Scope's murder.

"You don't think her son did it, do you?" he asked.

"I don't know whether he did it or not," I answered. "But if he did, I don't think he acted on his own. He's a little too far over-the-edge to be that decisive."

The eyebrows went up again.

"You think Tella pushed him?"

"I don't know," I said firmly, looking him in the eyes. "And I'm not making any accusations."

"For what it's worth, I'd argue against it. She struck me as too straightforward for that."

"Maybe she is. In any event, this is a police matter, and I don't interfere in police investigations."

"Good policy." He nodded with slightly mocking wisdom. "And the legal thing to do, I understand."

"Right."

Curtis insisted on paying for dinner, using the same line he had used for the drinks. I was too full and too comfortable to fight over the check, so I thanked him and let him pay as graciously as I could. It meant I owed him, though, and I wasn't too happy about that.

I declined firmly when he wanted to see me home.

"I'll call you," he said, shaking my hand.

I didn't tell him not to.

I walked home on automatic pilot, trying to figure out whether I wanted to have a real date with this guy or not and wishing I'd had sense enough to find out more about him personally, not just professionally. Things like where he came from, what brought him to Reno. So I didn't realize something was wrong until I was almost on the steps to the front porch. A dim light was glowing through my office window. The sun had been shining when I left. I hadn't turned a light on.

I slipped over to the driveway and moved quietly around the garage to the back of the house. Butch materialized next to me as I reached the kitchen door, and I saw Sundance sitting on the sill of the bathroom window, the one the cats use for access. Both of them looked ruffled, fur on edge.

I turned the key in the deadbolt, reached around the edge of the door and slid the chain lock loose. I stepped into the kitchen and shut the door behind me, leaving Butch on the porch. I didn't want the cats to give me away.

I placed my feet carefully on the linoleum, wishing I weren't wearing boots, wishing I had taken a gun, fearing that a detour to the bedroom to pick one up would give whoever was in my office time to get away.

If he hadn't already found one of the guns.

Or brought one with him.

The hall carpet muffled my steps. I leaned against the wall, listening, not certain what the best entry to my office would be.

"If you have a gun, put it down, Miss O'Neal," a male voice called. "I just want to talk, and I got tired of waiting outside."

"Who are you?" I asked from the hall, ready to head back the way I had come and sprint the two blocks to the police station if I didn't like the answer.

"Larry Agnotti," the voice said. "I think you knew my ex-wife."

I peered around the corner. The man sitting behind my desk had silver hair that matched the thread in his pinstriped suit. A paisley tie with a thick knot picked up the glow from my desk lamp. His features were thin and aristocratic, his skin pale.

He gestured toward one of the folding chairs I have for clients.

For the second time that evening, I couldn't remember how to sit.

"So what do you think about Gloria's murder?" he asked once I was settled. Under other circumstances, I would have described his tone as kind.

"I don't know anything about it, sir. I don't think anything about it," I said.

"You think Guy killed her? You think her son killed her?" he asked gently.

"I don't know, sir. Really. I don't know."

"Guy's crazy, you know that."

He waited. I had to answer.

"Yes, sir. I know that."

"I don't think he did it. I think somebody else did it, knowing Guy would be blamed. You think that's possible?"

"Yes, sir, I do."

I could feel perspiration forming on my upper lip, flowing down my ribs from my armpits, soaking my shirt.

"Good." Larry Agnotti smiled as if he had a razor between his lips. "And the person who's in danger next— let me know if you don't follow this—is Tella. On the one hand, somebody, the police, might think she influenced Guy and arrest her for murder. On the other, if she's not arrested, somebody not the police, somebody who might have decided the best way to end the fight over the company was to get rid of everybody in the family but Mike, the boy genius, might then feel the need to act again. With Gloria dead and Guy in the loony bin, Tella would be the target. You agree?"

"I agree." I didn't exactly agree, but I did follow his reasoning. Close enough.

"So someone may want Tella out of the way, right?"

"Right."

Actually, I had thought of that.

"I don't want anything to happen to Tella, Miss O'Neal. Listen carefully here." He leaned forward on my desk, gazing intently into my sweaty face. "The woman you know as Tella Scope is my daughter. I don't want anything to happen to her. So you are going to protect her, or you will be very, very sorry."

I opened my mouth to argue, but no words came out.

Chapter
6

LARRY THE LAMB made me an offer I couldn't refuse and left me with questions I couldn't get answered. He sort of took care of the "Why me?" question—he thought a woman could hang around close to Tella less suspiciously than a guy, and I was already involved. Not only that, but he wasn't happy that I had brought his name into it by nosing around. And thus complicated Tella's life. If somebody else found out she wasn't Ted Scope's daughter, my fat would be in the fire.

I didn't know whether Rudy had let something drop in Las Vegas, or whether Gloria had talked to Larry before she died. I figured I'd have a one-on-one with Rudy about confidentiality when this was over.

Larry also let me know I'd have a backup or two, which stopped the flop sweat from pouring down my body, although it didn't exactly dry it up. He wouldn't tell me who the second-stringers would be, or anything about them. Safer for me, he explained.

The depth of the coverage—along with the electronic security system—meant that I wouldn't have to move into the castle. I could come home at night.

He ordered me not to discuss him with Tella or with

anyone else—not even to mention his name again. And speculations about his relationship with Gloria and his lack of relationship with Tella were out-of-bounds. Larry and Gloria had decided that it was best for Tella to grow up thinking Ted Scope was her father, and he didn't want me to spoil their plan.

I told him I wouldn't dream of it.

The reward if I succeeded in protecting Tella until the thorny situations surrounding Gloria's murder and the future of the company were settled, and the punishment if I failed to do that, were both nebulous. Nevertheless, I had the feeling that both were substantial.

I didn't have a chance to tell him that I was a lousy bodyguard, I'd lost the only client who had hired me in that capacity, and I didn't want to get back on this particular horse that had thrown me.

I also lacked a cover story, given that I couldn't even mention his name to Tella, to explain why I was going to accompany her to work. Larry the Lamb thought that was my problem.

I tried to probe him about Gloria's murder, but it was a clumsy attempt. He wouldn't discuss it, except to emphasize that all I had to do was protect Tella.

When he was finished telling me what he wanted, and certain I understood, Larry got up from my desk chair, nodded politely, walked out my office door, and disappeared.

I sat in the folding chair, staring at my leather desk chair, empty except for a shadow, and wondered if I could ever take my place in it again without thinking of Larry the Lamb.

My home, my security, my sense of self had all been violated.

Something brushed against my ankle. Sundance, shivering. Butch jumped up on the desk, fur puffed defiantly, tail twitching. He stalked it twice for enemies before settling under the lamp, and even then he was checking the corners with dilated pupils.

They were braver than I was, but I didn't want them to know that. If they could move, so could I.

"Come on, guys," I said, needing to crack the silence with my voice. "There must be a couple of cans of kitty tuna in the kitchen."

They trotted ahead of me down the hall, settling slowly back to normal. I managed to open the cans and dump them into dishes before the smell and the stress got to me.

I lost the undigested prime rib in the toilet.

The night was a long one. I kept waking up, hoping for inspiration, discovering only anxiety. About three a series of thumps punctuated by an occasional pathetic squeak told me that either Butch or Sundance had caught a small rodent in the kitchen. Or maybe caught one outside and brought it in to play with. They do that. Cats think it's good for the soul to batter mice to death by repeatedly tossing them in the air and letting them fall on the linoleum.

When I couldn't stand the sounds any longer, I got up, put slippers on, and confronted the cats in the kitchen. Butch was standing over the body of a field mouse, paw raised. Sundance was crouched a foot away, waiting his turn. The stiff little legs sticking up meant that I had held off long enough for them to kill it.

I grabbed a dustpan from the utility closet and scooped up the corpse. The two cats slinked after me, glaring, to the front door. I tossed the mouse out, and they went running after it, quickly deciding that I was only modifying their game.

My one bit of luck that night was that they didn't find it and bring it back in.

I went back to bed, resigned to going with the sole excuse I had come up with to justify hanging around Tella for a while—the Protestant work ethic, lame as it might sound. I would insist on being her bodyguard in order to work off the retainer she had paid me.

Rather than allow her the opportunity to turn me down over the phone, I gave in to my insomnia at dawn, got up, took a shower, and drove to the castle, stopping briefly at McDonald's to pick up coffee. I probably wouldn't have made coffee anyway, but the kitchen still smelled of death.

I don't often see the sunrise. The last memorable time I watched the early glow in the eastern sky, I was escaping from an armed fortress, which was only slightly more stressful than having my future depend on keeping Larry the Lamb's daughter safe.

I parked the Jeep across the street from the entrance to the driveway and drank my coffee. I couldn't see any signs of life, and I wondered if Larry the Lamb had somebody in place on the premises. I'd have to ask Tella about the household staff.

The day was warming up, the green hedge had a golden glow on the leaves, and several cars had passed down the street before the teal BMW with the license plate CHIPS2 rolled out of the drive, with Tella at the steering wheel. I watched the car all the way to Plumb Lane, and only started the Jeep after she turned left. I didn't see anybody else.

Nobody paced us down Plumb to Kietzke, nobody was following as the BMW took Kietzke to the Scope Chips site. If Larry the Lamb's backup bodyguard was around, he had some kind of deep cover.

I caught up with Tella and beeped my horn as she was

waving to the man in the gatehouse. She rolled down her window, said something, and he nodded. The crossarm stayed up for both cars. She parked the BMW in the space next to the front door, and I parked the Jeep in the adjoining space.

She was standing beside her car, waiting, when I got out of mine. This time she was wearing a hot-pink jacket and skirt, still with white silk blouse and gold chain.

"What's this all about?" she asked. "I would have called again. You should have set up an appointment."

"Can we talk inside?"

"Come on," she said.

I followed her through the front door into the reception area.

Tella and the keeper of the inside gate exchanged pleasantries, and we were buzzed through to the open area. Only two people, a man and a woman, were at their desks. They each greeted Tella with a brief hand wave and kept working. Tella said nothing until we were back in her office, in her territory.

The chair she pointed to was more comfortable than the one I had been sitting in the night before, but I was just as aware of the power discrepancies. The difference was, I wasn't afraid of Tella.

"Now," she said, leaning back comfortably. "I spotted you at the light on Virginia Street. Why did you follow me to work?"

"Because I thought somebody should, and I'm still in your employ," I replied. "If your brother Guy did bash your mother—and I don't know if he did—then somebody whispered in his ear. And with Guy and Gloria both out of the way, that only leaves you before the company's up for grabs. Unless your brother Mike wants it all for himself."

She didn't say anything, so I continued. "I want to work off the retainer as your bodyguard. For as long as you need me."

That sounded better than I had feared. And it was close to the truth.

Tella nodded. "Good. We're thinking along the same lines. But I don't want a bodyguard. I want you to find who really killed my mother. I don't believe my brother did it. If he had, he would have told me."

"Did he tell you anything?" I decided it was best to find out what I could. We could come back to the bodyguard question.

"He said he saw a spaceman in the backyard. He said he was looking out the window, watching Daddy's ghost, and a spaceman landed. He was afraid the man was coming to take him back to the ship, so he closed the blinds, locked the door, and turned out the light. He didn't talk to anyone until morning, when he felt safe again." Tella leaned her face against her hands, elbows on the desk. "I knocked on his door when I came back from the library. When he didn't answer, I just thought he had gone to bed early. Of course, he thought I was the spaceman."

"He was watching the ghost when the spaceman landed?" I had a little trouble with that. "Since the police don't believe that, they think he wasn't in his room, that he was out waiting to bash his mother in the backyard."

Tella nodded without looking up.

"Did anyone see your mother go outside?" I asked.

"No. But she must have gone out almost immediately after you left. She had been dead for hours when Jorge found her in the morning."

"Jorge's the gardener? Does he live with you?"

"He comes twice a week, Tuesday and Friday. We have a

live-in housekeeper, Beatriz, but other than that, it's just family."

"Neither Beatriz nor Mike heard or saw anything?"

"Beatriz was in her room with the television on, and Mike wasn't home. He was here, working. Sometimes he stays here, even though he can work just as easily from the terminal in his bedroom."

"Does he have one of those workstations?"

"No. His office has a door, just like mine."

"How long has Beatriz been with you?"

"Years. I was just a teenager when she came."

If Beatriz was also employed by Larry the Lamb, she had to be in deep trouble over Gloria's murder. If she wasn't, then who was going to be protecting Tella at night?

"All right. Let's figure out how we're going to keep you safe. I can't do anything if you won't cooperate."

"I recognize there's a possibility that someone will come after me—although I think it's remote. I think it's far more likely that I'll be named as Guy's accomplice, either by the phone or by the rumor mills, and the innuendo will cripple my ability to run the company." Tella lifted her face and smiled. "I forgot to thank you. You obviously don't think I incited Guy to murder our mother. I appreciate that."

"Not a problem," I told her. Besides, until I talked with my late-night visitor, I thought she might have done just that.

"Good. Then you must see that the best thing you can do for me is to find out who the spaceman was." I must have looked startled, because she added, "Guy saw something— make that someone—in the yard. The spaceman must be the murderer."

"Tella, I can't poke around in a police investigation. I could lose my license." Not only that, but Larry the Lamb surely had somebody else working that end of it, and if something happened to Tella, who was now my responsibility, I could end up in even more trouble.

"I thought of that. I don't think it would be a problem, because they're not doing much investigating. They think Guy did it. But we'll still have Guy's lawyer retain you as part of the defense team."

"Who's his attorney?"

"Pam Calloway, for the moment, although we're evaluating our choices in criminal lawyers, in case you don't find the spaceman before Guy goes to trial."

Finding the spaceman sounded like a long shot. But the alternative was protecting Tella until Larry the Lamb decided she was safe and called me off.

"Are the police trying to hang the rifle shots at graduation on Guy, too?"

"They haven't filed charges on that one. I don't think Guy was there, but he may not have an alibi. He spends a lot of time alone in his room."

"Hiding from aliens?"

"I'm afraid so." She expelled her breath sharply, as if she knew how that sounded.

"Okay. I'll look into the murder. But on condition we work out a plan for your protection at the same time."

"What do you want me to do?"

"How's this—I come with you to work in the morning, look for the spaceman as long as you're safely in the office, and come back to see you home at night. Anywhere you go that isn't home or office—meals, parties, meetings on somebody else's turf—I go with you. You tell me your schedule each day, and you don't deviate."

"I think it's silly. I think it's a lot of work for you, baby-sitting me, without any clear payoff."

I thought the same thing, but I wasn't willing to risk Larry the Lamb's wrath any more than I had to.

"But if you insist," she continued, "that's how we'll handle it."

"I insist." I discovered I had been gripping the arms of the chair. I relaxed my fingers. "So what does your day look like?"

"I'll be here all day. I'll ask Chareese to bring me lunch at my desk. I do that sometimes, so no one will think it odd."

"Chareese?"

"You met her. The woman at the front desk. Be back here at six and we'll leave together, grab a bite of dinner, and then meet with the creator of *Oh, Nevada*. He wants to talk with me about continuing to back the show."

"You're kidding."

She laughed sharply. "Not at all. Memorial to my mother, and all that."

I didn't have words to deal with that.

"Is there another memorial? A funeral service?"

I was embarrassed that I hadn't thought to ask before. But Tella wasn't exactly crippled with grief, if that was any excuse.

And she had the grace to look distressed by my question.

"We'll do something. We haven't decided what's appropriate. Anyway, the coroner hasn't released the body."

I almost wished I hadn't asked.

"When do you hear about the autopsy?"

"The results will be available sometime today." She shifted uncomfortably in her chair. "The preliminary hearing is tomorrow morning. I haven't decided whether to go."

"I don't understand. Won't Guy want to see you there?"

"Yes—but I don't want to face reporters, for one thing. And for another, if he makes too much of a fuss, wanting me with him, it'll just look worse for both of us. Besides, Pam says the judge is going to refuse bail and send him for a psychiatric evaluation. And I don't really want to watch that happen."

"How can you work with all this going on?"

Tella shut her eyes and burrowed down farther into the chair. "Because I have to. We have a contract to fulfill, bugs to work out of the second-generation chip, by June thirtieth, the end of this month. Everybody who can write code is writing code. The murder and Guy's arrest have already shaken investor confidence—the NASDAQ quote on Scope Chips' stock dropped two points yesterday. If we blow the deadline, we could still be facing a proxy fight."

"Your mother was murdered, your brother was arrested, and nobody's going to cut you any slack?"

"Not in this business." She managed a weak smile. "But thanks for caring."

"You're welcome. I'll see you at six." I stood, then stopped before I got to the door. "Your brother Mike. Is he here today?"

"Probably not yet. You'd be better off catching him this afternoon. Where are you going now?"

"To see what I can find out about Tom Warfield."

"I don't think he's direct enough to murder someone. But it's your job, I'll let you do it."

"Thank you."

We smiled at each other. I was starting to like her at last.

"If you want to talk with him, he'll probably have lunch at the Comstock Room. He has a table reserved every day, just in case he decides to use it."

"Thanks for the suggestion," I said. "I'd be surprised if he turned out to be the spaceman. Or either of the other two outside board members. But the first question to ask when someone is murdered is 'Who benefits?' And in truth, you're the obvious choice."

Tella nodded, with the same grace she showed earlier.

"After you," I continued, "it's the three guys. So I have to check them out."

"See you at six," she said.

"I'll be back a little earlier than that, to talk with your brother. Could you arrange something with Chareese so that I don't have to disturb you with my comings and goings?"

"I could, but I think I'd like to know when you're here. I will tell her that you're welcome. And I'll tell the guard at the gate as well."

The door clicked open, to let me out. I felt that a ceremonial bow was in order, or a salute of some kind. I gave Tella a small wave of the hand and left.

I crossed the quiet room to the front window, and Chareese buzzed me out, appraising me with large dark eyes in an intelligent face. I'd talk with her when I got back. Surely I would have to wait for Tella, and the timing would be better then.

Besides, I'd been up for a long time, operating on no more than a cup of McDonald's coffee. I was ready for breakfast.

The guard at the gate nodded to me as he raised the crossarm to let me out. I was willing to bet he had checked the Jeep's license plate with the DMV, and I wondered if he knew Larry the Lamb.

I drove back along Kietzke to Moana Lane, cut across to Virginia Street, and drove through another McDonald's for an Egg McMuffin and more coffee. I propped the coffee against my crotch and ate the sandwich as I headed toward the *Herald* office. When I managed to get there without spilling coffee on my leg, I decided the day might be picking up.

I wasn't expecting to find anything incriminating in the newspaper morgue, but I might find something useful, and it would fill the time until I could expect Tom Warfield to leave for lunch. Tella was right. I was more likely to get a positive response if I accosted him on the street than if I tried to get into a home or an office.

Good luck on all counts.

Two hours of reading microfiched newspaper articles gave me a headache, and not much more. I had had a vague sense going in that Warfield had barely escaped a criminal indictment in the late eighties, and I had wanted to refresh my memory on that. But it was hard to tell just what had happened.

Several colleagues of his had been charged with mail fraud and violation of Securities and Exchange Commission rules on insider trading and had plea-bargained their way out of trials and into very short jail sentences. Warfield was aware of what was going on, but no one could prove he took part. He had claimed that it was all a politically motivated witch hunt, and that nobody had done anything really wrong.

I suppose that depends on your definition of wrong.

Warfield had ended up barred from the securities industry for five years, which were now up. He had spent those years building up his good name in Nevada, serving on all the right committees and attending all the right fund-raisers. He had crossed paths with Harding and Zabriskie socially before they joined the board of Scope Chips, but there didn't seem to be a long-standing business connection.

I found one picture of the three of them together, labeled. When I had seen them at the theater, I had had the feeling they all looked alike. With names attached, I sorted them out.

Warfield was the tallest, with the whitest hair and the squarest jaw. Harding had a glass in his hand, and the lack of focus in his eyes led me to believe he'd had more than one. Zabriskie was the only one smiling. He had salt-and-pepper hair, the youngest of the three.

If either Harding or Zabriskie had had a problem with the SEC, or any other government agencies, it hadn't made the *Herald*.

A little before noon I wandered over to the Mother Lode. The Comstock Room was the restaurant on the seventh floor, and the only way to get there was via the elevator just inside the front air curtain of the casino. The Mother Lode, like most casinos, doesn't have doors because it doesn't close. The air curtain keeps out winter snow and summer sun.

I didn't really think Warfield would go to lunch that early, but I wanted to spot him whenever he came in. I got five dollars in quarters from a change girl who looked as if she had just graduated from high school. The black fishnet stockings covered legs that wobbled in their first high heels, and nothing but hope held up her bustier. If she had met my eyes, I would have told her to go to college, but she didn't look up as she clicked the quarters into my hand.

Playing quarter slots isn't how I would choose to waste a couple of hours—I'd rather play Keno. But since the slots and the blackjack tables were the only places to wait with a view of the elevator, I found a machine that looked promising and plunked in a quarter. I did it slowly, wanting to make the quarters last, even though I could put them on my expense account.

I don't win often at Keno, and I didn't expect to see the

quarters again, once they went into the slot. Whenever you walk into a casino and put your money down, it's a bet against the house, and the odds are always with the house. In the long run we're all dead, but the house is a winner.

Keno is a bad habit, though, hard to break even if I tried. The feeling sneaked up on me, over years of playing a game or two now and then, that the next game might be the big bazooka, the chance of a lifetime that would set me free. Free from something, I'm not certain what. If I don't play, maybe I've thumbed my nose at the gods, just as they decide to smile on me. And I'm afraid if I really played the slots, the same thing would happen. I'd start to think the next quarter would do it, that I could bet against the house and win. So I play an occasional game of Keno, remembering the house has the odds, and stay away from all other games of chance.

The quarters were still holding out when I saw Tom Warfield—tall, white haired, and square jawed, just like his photograph—walk through the air curtain and over to the elevator.

Playing slowly, winning a few back every now and then, I lost a full five dollars in quarters waiting for him to come back down. He had been alone on the way up, but Zabriskie stepped out of the elevator right behind him. I had missed Zabriskie's ride up, but then I hadn't been watching for him. He should have been easy to spot—he and Warfield were the only two men in suits and ties in the whole casino.

I grabbed the last couple of quarters from the payoff tray, stuck them in my pocket, and followed the men through the air curtain to Virginia Street. I wanted to accost Warfield alone, if possible, rather than try to talk with them both.

But Warfield started to turn left on the sidewalk, then stopped so short to light a cigar that I almost ran into him.

He glanced up from the flame and caught my eyes before I could look somewhere else.

"Miss O'Neal, isn't it?" he asked between puffs.

"That's right, Mr. Warfield," I answered, wishing I could back up a step or two. The cigar smelled sweet and heavy, and I resisted an urge to grab it and stomp it out.

"I thought you might make contact. Ross, say hello to Miss O'Neal."

Zabriskie dutifully smiled and held out his hand. I shook it, and we exchanged polite greetings.

Warfield puffed on the cigar until he got it right, then he smiled, too. The teeth had to be capped. At his age, smoking cigars, probably drinking coffee, too, the gleaming white of his incisors couldn't be natural. His skin reminded me of clay. His eyes, though, were what defined him. They were dark and had an edge to them, as if something inside them was sharp enough to cut.

"You did a nice job protecting Gloria at the graduation ceremony," he said. "Too bad you weren't at the house Monday night."

"Thank you, sir." I hoped no one ever told him that I was at the house Monday night.

"My attorney, Van Woodruff"—Warfield paused for a flickering instant to see if I'd react, but I didn't—"said he saw you at the party Sunday. He was sorry you left before he had a chance to talk with you."

"Gee, I wish I'd known that. I would have stayed," I said flatly.

"I'm sure." The smile was unwavering. "Van thought you might be concerned about Gloria's death, especially since you've lost clients before, also under questionable circumstances."

I resisted the almost overwhelming desire to tell him that

Gloria hadn't hired me. And add my opinion of Van Woodruff, who should be in jail for abetting a felony, not practicing law. The humble smile I offered Warfield made me think about barfing. Again.

"Murder is a little more than a questionable circumstance, sir." The words oozed out between clenched teeth.

"True, Miss O'Neal. Still, I don't think you need to worry about this one." He slapped a hand on my shoulder. I shrugged it off, still smiling. "We'll see that the boy gets help. He doesn't have to go to jail."

"That's assuming the boy is guilty." When Warfield's smile still didn't waver, I added, "What happens to the company?"

Warfield hadn't expected that question. He discovered his cigar had gone out and pulled the lighter out of his pocket. Zabriskie and I both waited until he puffed the disgusting piece of rolled tobacco leaf back to life.

"The company will do very well. Just as Ted Scope would have wanted. Better, even." He couldn't resist that.

"And Tella?"

"Well, there's no question that Tella is important to the future of the company, not to mention the fact that her brother Mike is going to need her, with all the disruptions going on."

He hadn't expected that question, either. "Disruptions" sounded even more distasteful than "questionable circumstances."

"Did Tella hire you, Miss O'Neal?"

Zabriskie asked that one, and neither Warfield nor I had expected it. I took another look at him. His skin had a healthier cast, and his eyes didn't have that edge. A softer man than Warfield, not necessarily less intelligent.

"I've been hired to help establish Guy Scope's defense,"

I said. They both stared at me. "Guy Scope saw someone in the yard that night, and I've been asked to find out who he saw."

Warfield started to chuckle, a sound that began deep in his throat. Zabriskie picked it up when it bubbled over.

"The spaceman?" Warfield asked. "You're looking for the spaceman?"

"That's right, Mr. Warfield." I looked him in the eye. The idea was so absurd that I didn't even try to defend it.

Warfield took his wallet out of his pocket, pulled out a card, and handed it to me.

"Here, honey." He said it between chuckles. "If you have some real questions, call and make an appointment."

I crumpled the card in my hand as I watched them walk away.

Chapter
7

"I WILL NOT put any money into any show in which the Indians are simple thieves and Julia Bulette's house is full of young, pretty chorus girls who love their work."

"But that's censorship!"

"It's not censorship. Write whatever you want. And find another investor."

I had somehow missed meeting Terence Deming, the creator of *Oh, Nevada*, at Gloria's party. Just as well. I wouldn't have liked him then, either. He exuded an amazing smugness, a confidence in the artistic value of his work that had been unaffected by the lack of either popular or critical enthusiasm. Which might have been understandable if it had been art, but this was musical comedy we were talking about, and no one—not even Andrew Lloyd Webber— could take it this seriously.

Deming was over fifty and overweight—when he leaned forward to confront Tella, the buttons of his plaid shirt barely held across the white one underneath. His glasses rested on the bags that padded his cheeks, almost obscuring round blue eyes. Salt-and-pepper hair that needed a dandruff-fighting shampoo fell almost to his shoulders. And he clearly didn't like dealing with a woman. I wondered if

Gloria had even noticed. She had been so enthralled with the Eilley Orrum story that his attitude might have zipped right past her.

Besides Tella and Terence Deming, Bud Herrick and I were the only two at the meeting, which was being held in the green room in the theater's basement. Bud, a kind, red-faced, white-haired man, was the director of the Reno Theatrical Society. Although he was also my friend Sandra's father, he never remembered me from one sighting to the next.

I wasn't having a good time. And it was the end of an unproductive day.

After Tom Warfield and his buddy had left me feeling like dog food, I had gone back to Scope Chips, only to find that Mike Scope had left orders that he wasn't to be disturbed—not unusual for him, I was told—and that Chareese was unwilling to be drawn out where the family was concerned. Everything she said could have come from a press release.

I had hoped I could get a sense of who else worked in the building. But I couldn't interrupt any of the small working groups—men in either short-sleeved white shirts with loose ties or sport shirts and jeans, women in either jeans or skirts and blouses with low-heeled shoes—and the few who left before Tella did were so purposeful that I didn't try to stop them.

Tella left her office a little before six and bid goodnight to Chareese.

"There's no point in taking both cars," she said as we reached the parking lot. "Leave yours. I'll bring you back."

"I want to end up at the castle."

She raised her eyebrows. "Is that how you think of it? My mother thought of it that way, too. She liked to hear it called the castle. All right. We'll leave your car there."

Maybe I'd exaggerated the resemblance. But I didn't think so.

I followed the BMW back the same way we had come in the morning. I left the Jeep in the gravel driveway and climbed into the passenger seat next to Tella.

"The autopsy report," I said as she turned the car around.

"The blow to the base of the skull killed her. As close to painless as you can get. She never even felt the water."

"Weapon?"

Tella shrugged.

"A matter for speculation. Maybe even the tile edge of the pool. And so the coroner's office is keeping the body. No memorial service for a while."

I couldn't tell how she felt about that. She paid a lot of attention to her driving, getting us onto Plumas, turning away from town, and then dropping down to Lakeshore Drive.

"Have you decided whether you're going to the hearing?"

"I'll let you know in the morning," she said. "But I wouldn't bet on it, if I were you."

Dinner with Tella was difficult. We ate at a small upscale coffee shop near Virginia Lake where the waitress knew her about as well as the one at the Mother Lode knows me. The hamburger was three dollars more than exactly the same thing at a casino.

Tella asked all the questions, and I couldn't decide how much I wanted to say about myself. But I didn't do a very good job of deflecting her probes. When we left the restaurant, I had a sense that I had told her more than I had intended, mostly about my relationship with Ramona. I had managed to stay noncommittal about men, although if I could have figured out how, I would have found out if she knew anything about Curtis Breckinridge. Bringing him up at dinner didn't seem the thing to do.

After dinner we went straight to the theater. We parked in the lot, went in the open front doors and down the stairs, where Bud and Deming were waiting for us. As far as I could determine, we hadn't been followed.

Nevertheless, I pulled the doors shut. I wanted to hear anyone who came in.

Tella had gone straight for the jugular, but Terence Deming fought back.

"Your mother thought the musical was charming and nostalgic," he said, evidently not happy with the idea of looking for a new investor. Sweat was forming on his upper lip. "She was committed to seeing the show on Broadway."

"I know that, and I know it is a great personal loss for you that my mother is dead." Tella smiled, as comfortable with the sweat as her real father would have been. "I'm sorry that I can't help you. Truly. But I am no more willing to fund this so-called work of art, which I find personally distasteful, than I would have been to flush Scope Chips down the toilet because that was where my father was taking it. If you want my money, change the show. If you don't want to change the show, ask someone else for money."

"So-called work of art!" Deming gasped, puzzled, as if he didn't understand how free enterprise works.

I considered telling him that Michelangelo had faced the same problem. But he would have taken it as a compliment, one I didn't intend.

"Tella's right," Bud said cheerfully. "She shouldn't pay for it if she doesn't like it." He was seated next to Deming on the worn sofa, under a series of posters advertising past seasons. Tella was in a chair across from them. I had been standing in a corner where I could watch the stairs.

Deming slumped, and Bud dropped a heavy hand on his shoulder.

"It's the artist's curse," Deming said. "This dependence on other people's money."

"We can find another angel," Bud told him. "Don't give up."

"Good luck." Tella stood, nodded to me, and started out.

I said a couple of quick good-byes, which were ignored, and followed her.

The car alarm hadn't gone off, and nothing looked tampered with. The BMW started smoothly, and Tella turned south on Sierra Street.

"You were pretty tough on Deming," I said.

"He's a big boy. He can handle a little rejection. And I could have been worse. I could have told him not to quit his day job." She glanced over to make sure I smiled at that.

"Thanks for controlling yourself. I just don't want you to incite—or insult—anyone to violence while I'm your bodyguard."

"I'll do my best."

"What would it take for you to decide that you really do need protection for a while?"

"I don't know." Tella was startled by the question, and I let her think about it as we passed from the dark, tree-lined area near the university, through the neon section of Sierra, across the Truckee, and back to a quiet part of town.

She started talking again right after the dogleg from California onto Plumas. "I didn't get along well with my mother, I know you're aware of that. In fact, I'm a little relieved that she's dead." She didn't wait for a reaction, which was a good thing. I didn't want to give one. "The problems didn't just start when my father died. As long as I can remember, I've had a sense that I made my mother uncomfortable. A sense that she didn't like me, that she wished I were someone else. She would tell me that she loved me, take care of me when I was sick, go through all the right motions, but we were never close. I used to fantasize that it was all a mistake, that someday my real parents would come to get me. I don't understand the feeling of not belonging now any better than I did when I was a child, but I learned to accept it."

Damn Larry the Lamb for swearing me to silence.

"What about Ted Scope? How well did you get along with him?"

"As well as anyone did. He paid for everything and ignored us all. I'm not sure he could have picked me out of a lineup before the first summer I worked for the company, answering phones and running errands. I learned double-entry bookkeeping as an excuse to spend more time there. By the time I graduated from college, I knew the nuts and bolts of the business better than anyone."

"Including research and development?"

Tella shook her head, keeping her eyes on the road.

"I have some limited skills in that area, but I am not the genius that my brother Mike is. And that's all right." She added it quickly. "We have different strengths, we complement each other."

"And you both recognize the need to take care of Guy."

I thought it was a statement of fact, but she was silent too long.

"I hope so," she said finally.

The BMW's headlights caught the inky green of the hedge surrounding the castle. Tires crunched on gravel as the car pulled into the driveway.

"Why did he read to you then?"

"What?"

"Ted Scope. Gloria said he read to you, when you were little."

She flinched as if I had swung a two-by-four.

"He did. But one day he stopped. I don't know why. Are you coming in?"

I could guess why Ted Scope stopped reading to her. But Gloria wasn't around to confirm it, and I wasn't certain whether Larry the Lamb would.

"Yeah. I want to talk to Beatriz, and if Mike's here, I want to talk with him, too."

"Fine. Mike's car isn't here, though. You may have to put that off again."

I decided to let the subject of Mike drop for the moment.

"And I still want an answer to my question—what would make you take the need for protection seriously?"

She turned to look at me, hands still on the steering wheel. The spotlight on the lawn caught her hands and formed a halo around her blond hair, but her face was in the dark. I could barely see the bright dots of her eyes.

"That's just it," she said. "I can understand why someone would want to kill my mother. Not that I wanted to—but she could be so casually cruel, so negligent in the way she devastated the person she was confronting. Whatever self-confidence I have, I have in spite of her. Mike's achievements have been in spite of her. Guy would be functioning better if she had ever found the right person to help him. And that's just the family."

She shook her head, as if to clear it, then continued more quietly. "So someone might want to kill her. But I can't conceive of why anyone would want to hurt me. I don't believe I've made that much of an impact on anyone. I guess it would take a lot for me to think I needed protection."

I had no way of dealing with all the pain slopping out,

filling the car as if it were floodwater. And the chasm between the way I saw Tella and Tella saw herself couldn't be bridged in this conversation.

I wished desperately that Gloria were still alive. I could have confronted Gloria, forced the issue. I almost damned Gloria, but jerked my head back to the car. She was dead, and I wasn't going to judge.

"Okay," I said, since I wasn't willing to argue. "Then all I can do is ask you to humor me. A favor, if you will. Allow me to protect you. Cooperate with me."

I hated to put it that way, but I figured she could understand favors.

She nodded. "I'll try."

We got out of the car, and Tella set the car alarm. I followed her to the heavy wooden doors, watched her first hit the combination on the security pad, then unlock the heavy deadbolt above the lion's head. We stepped into the central turret.

"Where's Beatriz?" I asked.

"Probably in her room," Tella replied. "I'll get her. You can wait in the library."

"Can't you just buzz her or something?"

"I could, but I don't buzz her room unless I'm too sick to walk."

We parted company on the Oriental carpet, beneath the martyred saint. I walked down the hall to the right, to the room where I had last seen Gloria, and Tella went in the opposite direction.

The library was cold and cheerless. I couldn't find a light switch, but the open door illuminated a path to the fireplace. I turned the key in the gas jet and was rewarded by a brief hiss and then a blue flame. Better than nothing. I sat on one of the low sofas, close to the tile hearth.

Tella came in almost immediately, followed by a short, heavy woman in a pale flannel bathrobe.

"Beatriz, this is Freddie O'Neal," she said, and then added for me, "I've told Beatriz you've been hired to help Guy, and she's to answer your questions."

"Hi, Beatriz. Would you mind if we talk alone?"

Beatriz and Tella exchanged glances. If there was a subtext, I couldn't pick it up. Tella left the room, and Beatriz moved to the center sofa, where she sat heavily.

"Tella has heard what I have to say. What is it you want?" Beatriz fixed me with the large, dark eyes of an Aztec princess. I thought Aztec because there was something about her square, jowly face that reminded me of pre-Columbian sculpture.

"I just want to go over it again. What were you doing Monday night?"

"I cleaned up the kitchen after dinner and went to my room. I watched television and went to sleep."

"I was here that evening." I waited for her to nod before I continued. "Did you hear me, coming or going?"

"No."

"Did you hear anybody else, coming or going?"

"No. I don't listen. I respect the family's privacy. I think privacy is important for people. Don't you?" Her eyes were as impenetrable as onyx.

"Yeah, sure. Except sometimes it's my job to violate people's privacy." I wished I had found a brighter light to turn on. The blue flame didn't illuminate much. "If you really want to help Guy, you may have to violate somebody's privacy. And if it's Gloria's, it won't matter, because she can't be violated anymore. Did Gloria sometimes go outside to meet someone late at night?"

Someone like Larry the Lamb, maybe.

"I watch television. I don't watch the backyard."

"Not that night, I know that. But you might have watched it another night."

Not a flicker from those eyes.

"How long have you lived with the Scopes?" I asked.

"A long time. Almost fifteen years."

"Then you know who I should talk to, who might be able to lead me to the person Guy thinks is a spaceman. I want to clear Guy of the murder. Do you want to help me?"

"I don't know anything that will help Guy. I love him, but I know he is crazy. I can't help that." Beatriz stood, moving to the edge of the couch so that she could look down at me. Even that close, I couldn't read her eyes. "If you want to do something good here, you just see that Tella is all right."

She left the room without saying good-bye.

Beatriz wasn't a likely prospect to be Larry the Lamb's agent. I just wished I had another one. I sat there in the semidarkness until Tella came in.

"Mike still isn't back," she said. "What do you want to do?"

"Can you check the office? See if he's coming?"

Tella moved over to a telephone on a desk I hadn't seen, hidden in a corner between two heavy bookcases, dwarfed by an unlit painting. She picked up the receiver and punched in a number.

"Mike, are you there?" she asked, and paused. "If you're not on your way home, call me." She replaced the phone and sat on the sofa across the hearth. "He doesn't always answer. But he does listen to the messages. My guess is that he's left the office, and he'll be here in a few minutes."

"Okay. When do you want to leave in the morning?"

"Do we have to do this, Freddie? It seems a ridiculous use of your time."

"We have to do this." The fire flickered between us. "You are on your own when you're in the house or at the office. The rest of the time, I'm with you."

She nodded, resigned. "If you want breakfast, be here at seven. Otherwise, I'll be ready to go at seven-thirty. The preliminary hearing starts at ten. If I decide not to go, I have a meeting with Guy's attorney at three, and I expect you to join us. That's it."

There had to be easier assignments. I can't face breakfast before ten.

"I'll be here before you leave." Beatriz probably made good coffee. That would be an incentive. I wanted to go home, since I had to be back so early. But before I left for the evening, there was one more thing to do. "Would you mind showing me the backyard? Walking the route that your mother took to the swimming pool?"

"Now? In the dark?"

"I'll want to see it again in the daylight. I'd just as soon see it first at night, under roughly the conditions that Gloria faced."

"Okay," she said, rising. "Follow me."

I waited while she extinguished the gas log, then followed her down the long hall. When we reached the center of the house, I realized that there were French doors on either side of the painted martyr. Tella first touched a security pad, then led me through the near set, onto a cement patio. I could just discern a white wrought-iron table and chairs to my left.

"Do you want me to turn on the lights?"

"Were they on Monday night?"

"No. But my mother knew where the pool was. She wouldn't have tripped on anything. You might."

The moon was up, and my eyes were adjusting. A glimmer several feet ahead—this was a big backyard—had to be the plastic pool cover. I couldn't see a flower bed, even though the night air was heavy with roses and honeysuckle.

I walked forward, stopping at the edge of the cement, and turned back toward the building.

"Who could look out and see what was happening?"

"As you're standing, my brothers' bedrooms are on the second floor to the right. Beatriz sleeps below them. My bedroom and office are at the end of the wing. My parents had the wing to your left."

"So Gloria could have looked out of her window and seen someone in the yard?"

"Any of us could—if we had been looking."

I turned again to face the yard and the pool.

"But it was dark. Whatever she saw—anyone saw— would have had to have been white, or lit."

Tella didn't respond.

"Would you turn the lights on?" I asked.

The switch controlled two spotlights, one illuminating the patio furniture, the other the pool. I walked across the grass to the pool, bootheels sinking deeply into the lush earth. I still couldn't see to the far end of the yard. The pool cover looked heavy, stuck to the surface. I decided to let it wait until daylight.

The spotlights were so bright that I had to keep my eyes down as I walked back to the patio. As far as I could tell, the windows were all dark.

Nobody there but Beatriz, who didn't appear to be Larry the Lamb's type.

"What about the electronic security? Is there anything to cover the backyard?"

"The fence is wired. Anyone climbing over would trip an alarm."

"Okay, that's enough for now."

"How long do you want to wait for Mike?" Tella asked.

"Has he had time to get home?"

"Easily, if he was already on his way."

"Then I'll pack it in for tonight. There's no real hurry."

She switched the lights off, temporarily blinding me again, before the glow from the French doors registered.

I remembered the Oriental carpet and wiped my boots on the cement before I reentered the house.

Tella walked across to the front door with me.

"Do I have your word?" I asked.

"On what?" She looked innocent, a swan in hot pink and white.

"That you won't go out of the house until I get here in the morning."

She frowned, but she nodded.

We exchanged good-nights, and I left.

The front lights were still on. The Jeep was parked south of the BMW, just out of the illuminated area. I hadn't quite reached it when headlights arced across the drive and I heard tires on the gravel. I stayed on the porch until a silver Ford Taurus pulled in on the open side of the Beemer. The lights clicked off, and Mike Scope got out of the car.

He was dressed in a short-sleeved plaid cotton shirt and khaki pants that fit as if he hadn't bothered to try them on before he bought them. His face twisted, puzzled, when he saw me waiting for him.

"Freddie O'Neal," I reminded him. "Your sister hired me. Your mother invited me to the theater. We met there. I'm sorry about your mother." I almost forgot to add that.

"Sure."

With my identity settled, he started to move past me. I reached out and barred his path.

"If you have a minute, I'd like to talk with you."

Mike's oily hair came to my shoulder. He had to look up to face me. And he was close enough that I could see his teeth. The greenish yellow incisors weren't created by the porch light. I thought again about genes, and about neglect.

"Is it short? I'm hungry," he said.

"Your sister told me you weren't home Monday night, that you spent it working at the office."

"Yeah, I do that a lot," he said.

"Do you come home in the middle of the night much?"

"Is it the middle of the night?" His eyebrows lifted, as if the idea startled him.

"Not yet, but it's getting there."

"I come home when I get hungry, and it's too late to call and get something delivered to the office. I can't do that when Chareese isn't there. I guess sometimes it's the middle of the night."

"Do you ever check the backyard?"

"What?"

I repeated the question, but it didn't help. Mike didn't seem certain that the house had a backyard.

"Do you have any idea what your brother Guy might have seen out there, something he might have thought was a spaceman?"

"No." That time I touched him. He had to look down. "No. I don't know what Guy thought was a spaceman. I never have." He looked back up at me. "Is that all?"

I let him go.

I drove home slowly and carefully. The strain of the last twenty-four hours, with little sleep, was getting to me. And I wished that I could see the picture on the top of the puzzle box.

This time I noticed when I turned the corner that the light was on in my office window. I didn't stop. I passed the house, at close to normal speed, checking the dark cars all the way down the block. Each one appeared to be uninhabited.

I went all the way around the block twice, trying to spot something unusual. The third time I parked on Mill and slipped my way around the corner from tree to tree, staying out of the streetlight.

And then I decided, what the hell, it was only Larry the Lamb.

I walked straight up to my front door and turned the knob. The deadbolt held. I unlocked it and threw open the door.

"Hello, Larry," I called.

No answer.

The desk light was on, but no one was in my office. Butch and Sundown came trotting out of the bedroom and settled next to each other in the hallway, just outside the kitchen door.

I knew I didn't need to check the rest of the house, but I did anyway. No one was there, not even in the closets or under the bed. Not even a dead mouse.

I fed the cats, trying to conjure up a situation in which I had left the desk lamp on in the morning. I couldn't come up with one.

All I could figure was that it was a reminder. Whether I could find his inside agent or not, he was around, and he expected me to do a job.

A professional could pick a deadbolt and even lock it again, given enough time. And I had been gone all day and part of the night.

The windows were secure, once I shut the bathroom window so that the cats were stuck inside for the rest of the night. I didn't think a person could get in or out through the bathroom window, but I couldn't risk it. I pushed chairs against both the front door and the kitchen door, so that anyone who jimmied the deadbolts would find one more barrier. Someone who wanted in badly enough could do it, but probably not quietly.

I went to bed, exhausted, after setting the alarm for six-thirty.

I must have dreamed that I stayed awake all night, because the alarm woke me up in the morning.

Chapter 8

MORNINGS ARE FOR early birds, worms, and farmers who have a north forty to plow before noon. I'd skip them if I could, and every once in a while I do. Knowing I had to get up, I struggled awake on this one, thanking God it was Friday. I don't always remember which day of the week it is, but I'd kept track the last couple of days. Tella couldn't possibly leave the house early on Saturday or Sunday. I begged whatever unknown powers exist for two normal mornings before I had to get up at six-thirty again.

I took a fast shower, grabbed a brown-and-white striped shirt and a pair of jeans, and left the house with my hair still wet.

Tella was waiting on the front porch—in a pale blue dress and a patterned scarf—when I pulled into the driveway. I would have called being outside the door a minor violation of our agreement, except that I needed another small favor. I wanted her to wait a minute longer while I got a cup of coffee for the ride.

"You'd better hurry," she said. "Beatriz dumps out what's left when I leave and makes a fresh pot for Mike."

Beatriz had her hand on the pot when I found the kitchen.

She wasn't happy about letting me borrow a mug, but I promised to have it back before nightfall.

The coffee sloshed onto my jeans as I guided the Jeep out of the driveway and followed Tella's BMW along Plumas to Mount Rose. Fortunately, the coffee had cooled enough so that I didn't have to scream.

I took a sip and discovered that I had at least been right about one thing. Beatriz made good coffee.

We nodded our way past the guard at the gate, and I followed Tella as far as the front door.

"What time do we leave for the preliminary hearing?" I asked.

She shook her head and dropped her face so that I couldn't see her eyes.

"I'm not going. And you don't have to unless you want to."

"Okay. What time do we leave for the attorney's office?"

"Two-thirty."

"And you'll stay put until I arrive."

She looked at me, composed again.

"As long as you're on time."

I watched her through the glass doors as she said hello to Chareese, waited for the inner door to open, and started across the room as the door swung shut behind her.

Chareese worked long days.

Even after the coffee, my head was groggy. I couldn't think of anything useful to do at eight o'clock in the morning.

I went home and dropped back down onto the bed.

This time the phone woke me up.

It was Curtis Breckinridge.

"I had a good time the other evening," he said. "I was

hoping we could get together over the weekend. Are you free for dinner tomorrow night?"

"I'm not sure."

"Oh."

His voice fell so far I thought for a second the phone had gone dead.

"I'm working on a case, and it's going to take me through the weekend, and I don't know right now how much time I'm going to be spending with my client."

"Oh." That one sounded a little better.

"How about lunch on Monday? I don't think that would be a problem." The words came out before I thought about them. I didn't want him to feel bad.

"That would be fine," he said. "Would you mind coming to the campus?"

"Not at all. But isn't it between sessions?"

"Yes, the nicest time. The students aren't there." He laughed at his own joke, even though it was an old one. Professors had been saying that forever. "I'm a little embarrassed to admit it, but the PC I use at home isn't connected to anything. If I want to send or receive on Internet, I have to use the one on campus. I go to the office once or twice a week when I'm working on something."

"I understand. The Student Union at noon?"

"Meet me in my office," he said. "First floor of what was once the School of Business Administration, now called Warfield Hall, second door to the right. Can you find it?"

"Are you kidding about the name change?"

"I don't think so, although my source was the faculty rumor mill. The word is circulating that we're getting a substantial donation."

"Congratulations. I hope it doesn't cost you too much."

"Well—there's an argument, of course, between finance

and management on exactly what the cost is. Finance points out that he wasn't actually convicted of anything, and he has a lot of practical information that could be of value to our students. But some of us think finance is blind to what might be called the nonmarket implications here. We feel we shouldn't be party to what is an apparent attempt to buy respectability. Not only that, but he's a bad role model, even if he isn't a crook." Curtis paused. "Do you want to hear all this?"

"I really do. But I have to go somewhere, and I'd like to let it go until Monday."

"Fine. See you then."

It was after ten when I hung up the phone, but I figured I'd still be on time for the preliminary hearing. Nothing in a courthouse ever starts on time.

As I walked the few blocks to the squat, concrete building, I was still thinking about Warfield. And wondering, if he wasn't a crook, just what he was.

Tella had been right about reporters. There were two television cameras with crews scanning sidewalks in both directions. I ducked my head and kept walking, up the stairs and through the doors. Nobody tried to stop me.

The courtroom—Judge Robert Markey presiding—wasn't crowded. One man was conspicuously taking notes. Even though it was quarter to eleven when I took a seat, I still had a half hour to wait before Guy Scope's case was called.

He came out with his attorney, a woman with a thoroughly competent appearance, who was evidently Pam Calloway. And Tella had been right about the hearing. With virtually no discussion, Judge Markey refused bail and ordered Guy sent to Lake's Crossing Center for psychiatric evaluation.

As the bailiff took Guy's arm to escort him out, Guy looked frantically around the courtroom. I tried to catch his eye, but I wasn't the person he wanted to see.

I walked home, picked up the Jeep, and drove to Scope Chips.

For comfort and convenience—Tella's—I parked the Jeep in the lot and rode downtown with her, and in the teal BMW. It was a dangerous thing to do. I didn't want to like that car too much. Wanting things—whether cars or love—is just a setup for disappointment.

She didn't ask about the hearing, so I didn't tell her that I went.

Pam Calloway's office was on the fourth floor of the same bank building that housed Woodruff, Wallace, Manoukian and Lagomarsino. I realized when I exhaled that I had been holding my breath as the elevator passed the third floor without stopping. If I were luckier than usual, I might get through this without renewing my acquaintance with Van Woodruff.

Calloway and Calloway—I found out later that her husband, Bill, was the other one—occupied a small suite halfway down the hall from the elevator. The tiny outer office held only a desk—unoccupied—and a matching chair and sofa. There was no window, and nothing else to look at. We waited, standing, until Pam Calloway entered from one of only two other doors.

"I'm sorry I kept you waiting," she said. "I was on the phone."

Pam Calloway looked even more competent up close, like the kind of person who did her homework and knew what was going to happen next. She had curly brown hair that was short around her face and fell to her shoulders in back. Heavy glasses balanced a square jaw on a face devoid of makeup. Her jacket and skirt were darker and less expensive than the kind Tella usually wore, and neither hung quite evenly from Pam Calloway's heavy frame. But the impression wasn't sloppy, just of someone who had more important things than clothes to worry about.

She ushered us into an office that inspired the same kind of confidence her person did. There were two bookcases that managed to appear both orderly and used, a wall of diplomas and awards, and a desk with a Lucite cube of family photographs, so that both Calloway and her clients could see that she had kids.

After Tella introduced me, we sat in a pair of straight-backed chairs covered in a fabric that had once been dark green but was now the shade of decomposing leaves. I knew Tella had chosen her costume—the dress—carefully. She always did. At a guess, she was signaling that she wasn't the one in charge here.

Pam Calloway leaned forward, hands clasped and resting on her desk.

"The hearing went as expected. Guy's on his way to Lake's Crossing Center. The word is, they find everyone competent to stand trial, no reason to think Guy will be an exception. Guerin's case—as far as I know, anyway—will be that Guy and your mother were arguing in the backyard, he shoved her, she fell against the tile edge of the pool, and he pushed her under the cover and into the water in a panic. Then he went back to his room and made up the spaceman story."

David Guerin was the Washoe County district attorney, a man who really wanted to be governor of the State of Nevada.

"That seems not only circumstantial but far-fetched," I said.

"You think a jury's going to believe that Guy was hiding from a spaceman?" Calloway asked.

"No, ma'am. I think we have to find the spaceman before they believe that."

"Good luck." She turned to Tella. "Guerin would probably accept a plea of involuntary manslaughter, and we ought to consider it."

"You mean Guy ought to consider it," Tella corrected. "But since he's innocent, he also ought to turn it down."

Pam Calloway nodded in understanding, if not agreement.

"If that's what you want. We'll talk about it next week, when we have the report from the county shrink," she said. "And we might want to balance that with one of our own. Is there anyone in town who has already examined Guy?"

"Is there anyone in town who hasn't? He's seen several psychologists and one psychiatrist, and I'm not sure whether any of them would be on his side."

"Think about which one you'd feel comfortable calling," Calloway said. She was still leaning forward, still calm, and I began to hope Tella would stay with her, not try to bring an outsider in. I had a hunch Pam Calloway would have a good effect on everyone involved.

"I'll think about it." Tella sighed. "Anything else?"

"Not now. I'll let you know when I hear something. Do you plan on trying to see Guy at the center?"

"No." Tella's face drained as she said it. "No, I don't."

We broke up the meeting awkwardly. Calloway and I both did our best to smooth it over, but Tella wasn't helping. Calloway saw us to the door, and we rode down to the garage in silence.

"You want to know why, don't you?" Tella asked, once we were in the BMW and heading south on Virginia Street.

"Why what?" I wanted to know a lot of whys.

"Why I'm leaving Guy alone." She faced ahead as she talked. "I think they call it tough love. The longer he's alone, the crazier he'll get. The district attorney will either have to get him help because he's crazy or let him go because he's crazy. I can live with either one."

"Yeah. I think they call it tough love." I waited until Tella was signaling for the turn into the driveway before I asked, "What are your plans for the weekend?"

"At the moment I don't have any. A quiet weekend at home is the only thing on my agenda. Whatever work I do will be from the PC in my home office." She stopped the car and met my eyes before she added, "And I promise to call you if I decide to go out."

"I'll trust your word," I said. I wasn't sure if I imagined it, or whether she flinched. "If I don't hear from you, I'll see you Monday morning."

I got out of the car and said good-bye.

This time, home was just as I had left it. But I was still uneasy, still aware of the recent violation. I could almost smell Larry Agnotti's presence, and I wondered how many times I would have to come home and find everything untouched before I would begin to feel secure again.

There was food for the cats, but none for me. I thought fleetingly of calling Curtis Breckinridge and telling him I was free for dinner. I didn't do it. As the sun was setting, I was walking back along Mill to Virginia. I wanted to talk to Deke.

Riding up in the escalator to the Mother Lode coffee shop, I still hadn't figured out how much I could tell him.

Much as I needed to talk about what was going on, I had not only client confidentiality but Larry the Lamb's confidentiality to worry about. I was going to have to play it by ear, hoping Deke didn't feel like probing too much.

My heart lurched for a moment when he wasn't on his customary stool.

Diane saw me standing and motioned me over.

"He's here," she said. "In the men's room. Are you drinking coffee or beer tonight?"

"Beer. Thanks."

I was annoyed at how much my face had betrayed, but that wasn't her fault. I sat down and marked a Keno ticket as I waited for Deke to settle in next to me.

"What brought you here? I thought you'd found a new place to have dinner. Diane and I just weren't good enough once you started working for the Scopes."

"Right, Deke. Next week I move into the castle. Just saying good-bye." His eyes got so narrow that I added, "Just kidding. It's a weird place, and everyone in it is nuts, with the possible exception of Tella Scope."

"Whoever stuck the girl with that name?" His eyes relaxed and his jowls quivered as he shook his head.

"I'd guess her mother, but I didn't ask." Not her father. Not her real father. I pulled out a dollar and looked for the Keno runner.

"Good thing you didn't take that bodyguard job after all. Isn't it?"

I waited until the runner took my ticket and Diane brought his steak before I answered. I didn't want his full attention.

"Yeah. I'm bodyguarding Tella, though."

"Why? Who's after her?"

I hadn't waited quite long enough.

"Maybe nobody. But I don't believe she was involved in her mother's murder—and I don't think her brother did it, either—so she may be the next target."

"Then what are you doing here? Why aren't you having dinner with her?"

"She's home, and there's a security system there."

"Who? Or are you trusting an alarm?"

Shit.

"I'm not sure. It's complicated, and I can't tell you all of it. Yet." None of this was helping. "But she promised she wouldn't leave the house without me, and I promised to try to clear her brother. That's the deal."

"How do you clear her brother?"

"I find the spaceman." I still had trouble getting that out. There had to be a better word.

"Spaceman? Is that who took a shot at the woman the day you saved her?"

"No. I don't know. Maybe I should be looking for the sniper instead." That was the better word. When Diane put a hamburger in front of me, I attacked it.

"Have you checked on rifles? Hunting licenses? Does this child Guy Scope shoot?"

"No sane person would put a rifle in Guy Scope's hands, which doesn't mean it hasn't happened. I just don't think so. But Ted Scope belonged to some kind of a hunting lodge, and it may be time to take a look up there."

"I would think so," Deke said, nodding.

"Is anything in season?"

"Rabbits. You can always shoot rabbits, even in June, when they're not full-grown. So be careful."

"I'm not a rabbit, and I'm full-grown and then some."

"Just don't wear brown around a hunting lodge."

"If I can find a red hat, I'll put it on."

"And don't poke fun at a man with a rifle in his hand."

"God, Deke, you're full of laughs tonight." The second half of the hamburger didn't taste quite as good as the first half. I watched the numbers for the Keno game light up. I lost.

"You'll be full of more than laughs if you stick your nose in the wrong person's business and that person has a shotgun."

"I'll be careful."

"Why don't you just stick with the daughter? If trouble comes calling at the house, you ought to be there."

"I'll be with Tella most of the time. But we have an agreement." I couldn't spell it out any further, and this time Deke didn't push.

He wanted to know more about the office security, and he wasn't happy with my answers there, either. Neither was I. But I couldn't get in touch with Larry the Lamb to ask what he thought, so I had to go with my own best judgment. And hope I was right.

We finished our meals and parted company. I was almost sorry I'd looked for him in the first place. He was raising doubts in all the places where I already had them.

I wanted to check out the hunting lodge in the morning, but I didn't want to trust Tella's word that she'd be in all weekend. I tried again to imagine Beatriz as a secret agent and decided I couldn't stay away for two days.

The house was quiet and dark when I got home, and the cats weren't jumpy. One day at a time this was going to get easier.

I picked up the phone and punched Tella's number.

"Checking up?" she asked.

"Not yet. I'll check up tomorrow, when you've had a day to get cabin fever. I'm calling to get directions to the hunting lodge you told me about. Ted Scope's private club." I couldn't refer to him as her father any longer. With luck, she wouldn't notice.

"It's at Fallen Leaf Lake. I don't know whether anyone but the caretaker will be there this weekend. You won't be welcome in any case, though."

"I know. I'm still going. I turn onto Fallen Leaf Road south of Lake Tahoe. Then what?"

"I haven't been there. All I can tell you is that the lodge is south of the lake, about five miles past the ranger's station. And there's a No Trespassing sign on the driveway."

"I hope there's only one. If I'm going to barge in, I want to do it at the right place."

"What do you expect to find?"

"If I'm lucky, a sniper. At least someone with a gun."

"Good luck." The doubt in her voice carried over the wires.

"I'll call when I get back."

I had to figure that Tella was in for the night and wasn't likely to leave the next day until she heard from me. But nothing felt good. I went through my new routine of locking windows and barricading doors, and even that didn't help me sleep. I was up three times in the night, stretching kinks out, doing my best not to disturb the cats, because I couldn't open a window to let them out if it meant leaving it open. Closed windows were my one small hope of feeling secure.

Or so I thought. I gave in about dawn after Sundance had been crying under the closed bathroom window for a good five minutes, and I opened it. I promptly fell asleep until nine.

The morning was so clear and beautiful that a drive to Fallen Leaf Lake seemed like the best idea in the world. Flying somewhere would be better than driving, but it wasn't an option at the moment. The Lake Tahoe airport is such a short hop from Reno that I had absolutely no excuse to take the Cherokee.

As I got dressed, I thought about what Deke had said. I didn't have anything red to put on. A white shirt with a blue denim jacket was as bright as I could get.

I headed south on 395, watching the billboards until I passed the turnoff to the Mount Rose Highway. I couldn't help thinking of my mother, since that was the route I took to Ramona and Al's cozy cedar chalet.

I wished I could compare feelings with Wynonna, even though she always looked too waxen and made up to have any. It had never occurred to me, when I had seen pictures of the Judds and wondered which one was the mother, that someday my own mother would appear even younger than Naomi Judd. Well, as young anyway. Nobody could look younger than Naomi Judd. Not even Cher, although I wouldn't mind hearing how Chastity handled that relationship.

But no matter how difficult things were between us—and despite her face-lift, they were better now than they had been at any time since I was about eight years old—I couldn't imagine wanting Ramona dead. I couldn't even imagine being indifferent to her death, which was all Tella seemed to feel. I felt sorry for Gloria, who died with only an ex-husband to care one way or another.

I wanted to find the sniper.

Carson City came and went, followed by the Highway 50 junction. I started the winding climb into the Sierras, through the sweeping vista of evergreens. The traffic was heavy enough to slow me down. A lot of people thought it was a gorgeous day to drive to Lake Tahoe. I hoped not many would head south to Fallen Leaf.

The cars were bumper to bumper and down to a crawl by the time a diamond-white flash of sunlight through the trees signaled that I had almost reached the lake. The last twelve miles along the shore to Stateline took close to an hour, and by the time I was surrounded by the neon giants, I was hungry. I crossed to California, where the high-rise hotels were abruptly replaced with small motels and fast-food stands, stopped long enough to pick up a hamburger and coffee, and drove the few miles to Emerald Bay Road against the traffic, which was converging from both sides toward the casinos.

Nobody but me made the right-hand turn. The trees were closing in on the narrow road by the time I found the sign that said Fallen Leaf Lake, with an arrow pointing left.

There are easily a dozen small lakes that have the good fortune to be west and south of Lake Tahoe—that is, on the California side. Not that I particularly like California. Too many people and too many taxes, with not much civilization to show for either. But since the only forms of gambling that are legal in California off the Indian reservations are horse racing and the state lottery—a peculiar government-sponsored form that is actually part of the tax structure—no corporate types have had any big incentives to despoil the watery wilderness.

Viewing the Sierras from a plane, which I have done often, I can imagine Noah's flood receding from the mountains, falling away down the slopes, and leaving large puddles behind. Next to Tahoe, the other lakes look as if they hold only a handful of water, although Fallen Leaf, the largest, is maybe two and a half miles long and a half mile wide.

There are some vacation homes and a scattering of bed-and-breakfast establishments on the California side of Tahoe, but once away from Stateline, the level of commercial activity drops sharply.

The Fallen Leaf Lake ranger station had a sign promising information about camping, but no one was there to hand it out.

I glanced at the odometer, kept a steady pace for four miles, then slowed to look for a private road with a No Trespassing sign. I found one at four-point-nine miles, drove on for another three-tenths of a mile, then turned back. The sign was on a chain between two poles, waving across the middle of a dirt road that had been smoothed and packed since the last of the spring snows had melted.

I got out to look at the chain, leaving the engine idling. It was welded to one post and padlocked to the other. The post on the right side was too close to a tree for the Jeep to make it through, but it seemed to me that I might be able to scrape by on the left side. The ground was soft for a foot or two, not enough to stall with four-wheel drive.

I eased the Jeep off the road, around the post, and back onto the narrow dirt trail, hoping nobody was coming the other way. The tall pine trees were pressing in on either side, letting the high sun through only in occasional patches. I needed the blue jacket as much for warmth as for visibility.

After a few hundred feet of meanders, the road ended at a clearing. A rectangular building that might be a hunting lodge, built with authentic log veneer, was dead ahead. A gleaming black Range Rover, a maroon Pathfinder, and a faded red Ford pickup were parked in front. I pulled in next to the pickup.

I didn't see or hear any signs of life as I walked up the stairs and crossed the wide porch to the front door. I knocked and waited. When no one answered, I rapped hard enough to bruise my knuckles. There was still no answer.

I had just started to turn around when the bullet zinged past my ear and hit the door.

Chapter
9

WHEN YOU HEAR the bullet, you know it missed you. But by the time you remember that, your automatic nervous system has already taken over. All it knows is fight-or-flight, and the eyes hadn't sent a suitable attack target to the brain. The adrenals were pumping, and my muscles knew what to do. I lunged for the railing and swung off the porch, crouching next to the stairs.

The lodge had been built on a slope, so that the edge of the front porch was maybe four feet off the ground. The supporting pillars were narrower than a torso, and the stairs hadn't been closed off. I was suddenly glad I hadn't worn red. Brown would have been better, but blue would make it in the shadows. I did my best to fade into one just under the porch and peer out at the same time.

Whoever had fired the gun had to be in the trees beyond the parking area. And he wasn't wearing red, either.

I waited. He was going to have to move first.

The adrenal glands had done their job so well that I had trouble staying still. I felt with my hands in the dirt next to the pillar. Dry pine needles pricked my skin.

The spaces between the pillars were partly covered with lattice, although the wood strips had probably been dropping off for a decade. My right hand grasped a fallen section, and a splinter pierced my thumb. The short, sharp pain drained a little of the fear.

I wasn't carrying a gun. I sometimes slip a miniature one into my boot, but I hadn't done that before driving to the hunting lodge. It would have felt like carrying coals to Newcastle, or something like that. Besides, a small gun isn't a match for a rifle, a shotgun, or any other weapon likely to be found in a hunter's possession. And a larger gun would have been as obvious as a red flag in front of a bull.

Since I hadn't heard a second shot, I figured the sniper couldn't tell where I landed. One of the parked vehicles must have blocked his view when I dived off the porch. Staying behind the remains of the lattice as much as possible, I began inching away from the stairs, toward the edge of the building.

Even moving carefully, I stirred enough dust that I had to stop and hold my nose, fighting down a sneeze.

But I had paused at the right point. I caught a glimpse down the alley between the Range Rover and the Pathfinder of a man stepping away from a tree. He was tall and lean, gray haired, dressed in khaki work shirt and jeans. A rifle rested easily against his hip, barrel pointed down. He was looking around, puzzled.

"You can come out," he called. "That was just a warning, to keep you away from the door. I wasn't trying to hit you."

Fear turned to anger. I was crawling around in the dirt under the lodge, sticky with sweat, itchy with adrenaline, and if that asshole wasn't trying to hit me, he was at least trying to intimidate me. And I had been intimidated enough in the last week to fill my intimidation cup for a long time.

I made it to the end of the lodge without being spotted. I could just see the man's heavy boots, because the Pathfinder both covered me and blocked my view. He was standing at the foot of the stairs, facing the house.

"Where'd you go?" he called.

I stayed low as I slipped away from the house and leaned against the front wheel of the Jeep, trying to catch my breath without gasping. I couldn't see the boots, but I could hear steps moving toward me. When they stopped, I leaned forward, my head just above the level of the bumper.

The man was bent over, looking under the lodge, the rifle hanging loose at his side.

I threw the whole weight of my five-foot-eleven-inch adrenaline-charged body at that rifle.

He didn't let go, but he went over, falling on his left shoulder. I rolled on top of him, keeping his left arm pinned. I had one hand over his on the trigger guard, the other on the barrel. I twisted the barrel up under his chin.

My face was inches away from rheumy eyes, pocked skin, and bad breath. I lifted the top half of my body away, carefully, holding the gun with both hands and keeping him pinned with my legs and hips.

"I said I wasn't going to hurt you," he whispered.

"You shot at me," I said evenly. "My daddy taught me never to shoot at something I didn't intend to hit. What did your daddy teach you?"

"It was a joke. I'm sorry." His eyes began to water.

"You didn't answer my question." I put more weight on the barrel, pushing on the soft spot under his chin. "My daddy taught me that guns weren't toys. What did your daddy teach you?"

"Guns aren't toys. He said that. He did. I'm sorry." The words were coming in short bursts. "Let me up. Please."

"Let go of the gun."

"You don't want to shoot me. That would be murder. You don't want to kill me because of a joke."

"No. It wouldn't be murder. It would be self-defense. You shot at me. You used deadly force against me, and I have a right to protect myself at the same level. If I want you dead, you're dead."

"Please."

He began to whimper, and I began to feel ashamed of myself for terrorizing a whimpering man. I pulled the barrel away from his chin.

"Just a joke," I said. "I'm not going to hurt you. But you have to let go of the gun."

"Tom!" The word came out as close to a scream as he could manage. "Tom!"

"Warfield's in the lodge?"

"Tom!" He wailed.

The door to the lodge opened. I looked over my shoulder without relaxing my grip on the gun.

Warfield was standing there in a plaid flannel bathrobe, cigar in hand.

"Miss O'Neal," he said. "I thought I told you to make an appointment if you had any more questions."

"Sorry. I didn't have the telephone number for the hunting lodge."

"Tell her to get off me and let go of my rifle!" the man in the dirt cried.

"What happened?" Warfield asked.

"She was trespassing! I fired a warning!" He had wriggled around enough to get his left hand free. He used it to cover the end of the barrel.

I nodded.

"Miss O'Neal felt threatened, Corbin. You let go of the

rifle." When neither of us moved, Warfield added, "Miss O'Neal won't hurt you. I promise."

Corbin slowly took his hands off the rifle. Just as slowly, I stood up, still holding on to the rifle with both hands.

"What now?" I asked.

"Why don't you bring the rifle inside? I would rather not host your visit for long, but I'm willing to take a few minutes to find out what brought you here." Warfield smiled at me. I didn't feel any more welcome than I had when I was shot at.

Corbin scrambled back and got to his feet, awkwardly brushing himself off. I gestured with the rifle, and he moved away from the steps.

"Farther," I told him. "All the way to the trees."

I didn't think he'd rush me, but I didn't want to be nervous about it, either. Corbin backed his way across the parking area, watching me as if he thought I might fire if he turned around. He should have realized that shooting him in the back would ruin my self-defense story.

Once Corbin was safely in the shelter of the pines, I walked up the steps. Warfield stepped aside so that I could enter the lodge.

The main room was filled with heavy Mexican furniture, all dark wood and bright colors. A stone fireplace took up one wall, and mounted deer heads dotted the others. Zabriskie was standing near a window. He nodded as I crossed the threshold. George Harding, the only other person in the room, was leaning against the stone mantel, glass in hand. Both men were wearing slacks and open-necked sport shirts, and neither looked ready for the trail.

"Have a seat, Miss O'Neal," Warfield said as he stepped in next to me.

"I don't think so. Thanks anyway." I would have been the only one sitting, and it wouldn't have felt good.

"I hope that means this is going to be short." Warfield was still smiling. He seemed to do it easily. "Still looking for the spaceman?"

"Not at the moment, although I may get back to that." I wasn't going to let him bait me this time. "Since there was one unsuccessful attack on Gloria Scope before she was murdered, I thought I'd try looking for a sniper instead."

"Then it seems your expedition was at least a partial success," Zabriskie said. He moved away from the window and took a seat on a red and black sofa. "As long as you don't think Corbin took a shot at Gloria Scope."

"Just who is Corbin?" I asked.

"Caretaker, lodge keeper, handyman. He lives here, keeps everything in working order," Zabriskie answered. "And he almost never has occasion to drive into Reno."

"Is he the only one with a hunting rifle? Or do all of you have them?" I asked.

The men looked from one to the other.

"I have several," Harding said. He swallowed a large gulp of whatever was in his glass. "I am the only one other than Corbin who actually hunts up here. I also renew my deer license annually. Now I suppose you think I'm the one who took a shot at her."

"I don't know who took a shot at her, sir. I just have a little trouble imagining that it was her son."

Somewhere in the lodge a toilet flushed. The three men looked at each other again.

"You have another guest?" I asked.

"Must be Corbin," Zabriskie answered.

I supposed Corbin could have come in some back way. I just didn't think so.

"Why don't you take that rifle with you?" Warfield clapped his hand on my shoulder. "Have the police check it, if that will make you feel better. When you've done that, we can talk again."

I knew I was being dismissed, but I was feeling too bruised and dirty to argue about it.

"Since you're offering, I will borrow the rifle. And thanks for the hospitality."

"Any time. Although I still think an appointment would be more appropriate, Miss O'Neal. You're less likely to be shot at if someone knows you're coming."

"I'll remember."

Warfield held the door for my exit.

I looked for Corbin as I crossed the porch, but he hadn't reappeared. The truck was still there. Either he was still in the trees, or he had in fact gone in through a back door. I still thought there was someone else in the lodge, someone they didn't want me to meet.

If I hadn't been shot at once already, I would have driven the Jeep a mile or so away and slipped back. But they'd be watching for me to do that, and I really did want to get the rifle checked, even though I didn't think it would amount to anything. I also wanted to get the splinter out of my thumb.

I didn't want to stop at the Fallen Leaf ranger station. Too close, too easy for someone to follow me and take the rifle back. The nearest friendly washroom would be Stateline. Or it would have been, except for the bumper-to-bumper cars.

The day had lost a little of its luster. The sky wasn't as bright, the water wasn't as blue, and I didn't want to be there.

I drove home with my thumb aching.

Despite the warning shot, I had trouble thinking of those guys as murderers. Sharpies, yes. Killers, no. They had too much to lose to be killers, and too many other ways of getting what they wanted. Violence was for desperate people, people who couldn't imagine other choices.

I walked in the door to my house, ignored the blinking light on the answering machine, tossed the rifle on my bed, stripped off my clothes, crammed them into the hamper, and turned on the hot water in the shower. I tweezed the splinter out of my thumb and stepped under the water, letting it run a long time on the back of my neck while I soaped the bruised places.

After I was dressed, dry, and a little more comfortable, I went back to the answering machine. The message was from Ramona. She said she really wanted to talk to me, and she wanted to know when I was coming to the lake. I couldn't return that call, because I couldn't tell her I had just come back, and I didn't want to lie to her. I had to wait until I could talk about coming up, or not coming up, with a clear conscience.

I picked up the rifle and left the house with only a twinge of guilt.

The police station is only a couple of blocks from my house, and I would have walked, except for the gun. I drove the short distance to the parking lot and got out very carefully, rifle pointed at the ground.

Danny Sinclair was at the desk, a man who was going to turn out to be a career sergeant, and not happy about it. Not even in Reno was he considered smart enough to make the leap to detective. He had thinning red hair and a freckled face that turned a blotched color when he saw me. We hadn't liked each other in high school, and nothing had happened since to make either one of us reconsider. The fact that his name was the same as my father's probably hadn't helped our relationship.

I placed the rifle on the counter. Danny just glanced at it. "What's up, O'Neal?"

"I need to talk to Matthews. Is he in?"

Matthews was the detective who had interviewed me after the graduation day sniper incident. He had a kind of relaxed attitude about my ability to be in the wrong place at the right time, or vice versa, and I appreciated that.

"Not today." Danny didn't touch the gun.

"Well, then, maybe you could keep this rifle in a safe place until he gets here. Then ask him to check it against the bullet fired at Gloria Scope."

"No use checking for prints, is there? Looks as if yours would be all over it."

"Ah, damn it, Sinclair, I should have thought of prints. I'll remember next time. Thanks for mentioning them."

We glared at each other.

"Where'd you find this?" he asked.

"Stumbled across it by accident. Somebody must have left it for me." Telling him it was none of his business would have been worse.

"I'm sure Detective Matthews will want to call you," he said. He picked up the rifle with two fingers on the edge of the trigger guard, smiled at me, and walked away.

I almost yelled at him, but then I remembered the line about never arguing with a fool. I walked through the glass doors and the steps to the parking lot, feeling like a fool anyway, because I was going to have to drive two blocks home.

Once there I called Tella, to bring her up to date.

"I'm sorry someone threatened you," she said. "Why didn't you file a complaint while you were at the police station?"

"The hunting lodge is in California, so I would have had

to file a complaint there. Trying to find a sheriff's station and pressing charges would have been more trouble than it was worth. Besides, I was trespassing, and Corbin didn't know who I was, so I just don't see that anything would have been gained. I would have felt a little more like revenge if he'd hit me. As it turned out, we were probably about even."

"Threatening him with his own gun was revenge. Filing a complaint would have been upholding the law."

"You're right. And I didn't do it. And I'm not sorry. Do you want to fire me?"

"No. I still think you know what you're doing, even though I might not agree with it."

"Thanks. In that case, I think I ought to come over, spend the rest of the weekend with you."

Tella paused so long before she answered that I began to wonder if she'd floated away with the spaceman.

"You really don't need to do that. I promised I would stay in the house, and I will. I won't even go into the backyard. If you were here, I'd feel the need to entertain you." She overrode my attempt to object to that. "I'd be constantly aware that things are different, that my mother is dead, I'm in danger of losing the company anyway, and you think I'm in danger of losing my life. I would really rather be alone."

"Do you mind if I call every couple of hours or so?"

"No, of course not. As long as you don't mind if I'm short with you. The calls may become intrusive. I plan to work."

"Talk with you later."

I hung up with a mixture of guilt and relief. Tella would stay in the castle, and Larry the Lamb wouldn't hold me responsible while she was there.

Tella's decision also meant that I was free for dinner. And I didn't want to talk to Deke again.

I called Curtis Breckinridge.

"Is it too late to change my mind about dinner tonight?" I asked.

"Not at all." He sounded so pleased that I didn't know how to handle it. "Shall I pick you up at seven?"

"Why don't I meet you at the Comstock Room?" That was the first place that came to mind. The thought of waiting for somebody to pick me up—not to mention letting him drive—terrified me. The best I could do was meet him.

"Fine. That would be fine."

"And I'll still be in jeans."

"Wear whatever you like. I'm comfortable in jeans."

"Okay. But remember—this time I asked you."

He laughed. "Well—we could argue timing, who really asked whom—but I accept."

I hung up, feeling almost relaxed after all the shit that had come down.

I was fine, in fact, until I was ready to leave the house, when I had a sudden attack of agoraphobia. The last time I had had dinner with Curtis, I had come home to face Larry the Lamb. Not only that, but this time dinner was a real date, and not once in my life have I ever been comfortable on a real date.

Dating successfully is a skill, one that's easy to acquire in high school and becomes progressively harder to learn as you get older. Like foreign languages. Kids have no trouble picking them up, but the part of the brain that handles that function seems to atrophy with adulthood. To me, datespeak is a foreign language, like French, and I could never get the accent right.

I paused at the front door, trying to come up with some action I could take to help me feel more secure. I had done the best I could with the house. But a pro who wanted in wouldn't be stopped, I knew that, too. There isn't any way to stop a professional who wants in badly enough. I had to hope that Larry the Lamb didn't plan to deliver any messages while I was out.

As far as the date with Curtis Breckinridge was concerned, all I could do was plunge ahead. If we were both miserable, I could cut the evening short.

Walking down Virginia Street to the Mother Lode on a pleasant June evening was so familiar that I was almost calm when I got there. Taking the elevator to the seventh floor only rocked me a little, mostly because it was so crowded with couples. I hadn't expected that. I had forgotten what Saturday nights are like.

Curtis was standing next to the mirror across from the elevators, wearing jeans and a sport jacket. He smiled when I got out.

"I wasn't sure if we would need reservations, so I went ahead and made them. I'll just let the hostess know we're here."

Reservations. That was a word in datespeak. It would never have occurred to me to make reservations.

I watched Curtis talk to the hostess, a woman dressed in a red and black costume appropriate for the *Oh, Nevada* chorus line. He was nice looking, with the emphasis on nice. The smile lines in his face were permanent. And he wasn't sensitive about his hairline, or at least he didn't do any of the dumb things men do to try to hide it—no combover or sweep around of a few long strands. He just brushed it straight back. The sides were longer, curling around his ears. Comparing him with Professor Hellman, or others I had taken classes from, Curtis had style and confidence—a better interface with the rest of the world than most professors I'd had contact with.

He edged his way back to me, past the half dozen couples pressing toward the entrance.

"Just a short wait," he said. "They're setting up the table now."

I smiled, unable to think of a thing to say.

I had always hated the faux nineteenth-century look of the Comstock Room, and standing there under a huge crystal chandelier waiting for a table wasn't helping. There must have been a better place in Reno to have dinner on a Saturday night, one that people who dated knew about. Tella would have known—Sandra would have known—but it would have embarrassed the hell out of me to have asked either one and then had to answer questions about my plans for the evening.

Fortunately, the hostess waved menus at us almost immediately. Curtis was on one side of me, a mirror that tinged everything it reflected with the blood red of the wallpaper was on the other, and I was pressed so close to the woman in front of me that I could smell her bath powder.

From agoraphobia to claustrophobia in less than an hour.

Once we were seated at a table for two in the center of the room, I discovered another dilemma. I had what was certain to be an uncontrollable urge to ask for the Keno runner, which meant explaining to Curtis that I suffered from what is considered in Reno to be an undesirable habit.

Best he discover it early. I pulled a ticket from the stand next to the small lamp and marked eight numbers at random, added a dollar from my wallet, and held it up so the runner could see.

"What are you doing?" Curtis asked.

"Playing Keno. I do it a lot."

"Really? I was told that natives don't gamble. Or at least not regularly."

"Most don't, for the same reason that heroin pushers stay clean. They know the dangers."

"Are you saying you're an addict?"

His brow furrowed in a manner so sincere, so concerned, that I had to think about my answer.

"I'm not certain where the line is between a bad habit and an addiction. I know playing Keno is a habit, because I want to do it every time I come into a casino. I'd say it isn't an addiction, because I don't seek out casinos in order to play, I seldom stick around after dinner for another game or two, I don't lose any more now than I did ten years ago, and I don't bet the mortgage money."

Curtis relaxed his brow. "I'd say you're right. It's a habit, not an addiction. Although it's probably, over ten years, been an expensive habit."

"I wouldn't argue that." I sighed, wishing I'd skipped the game after all.

A Keno runner in a black bikini cut bodysuit and fishnet stockings, topped with a tie-on, fall-away skirt, plucked the ticket and dollar from my hand without stopping.

A demurely clad waiter popped up right behind her. I ordered prime rib, a rare treat for the second time in one week, and this time Curtis ordered game hen.

"The game hen is strong enough to handle red wine," he said. "Can I talk you into trying some?"

"Sure." I thought that was the correct datespeak response, and red wine wouldn't hurt me.

Curtis checked the wine list and ordered a bottle of California merlot.

"It's a light wine, good if you're just starting reds," he told me.

"You don't like beef?" I asked once the waiter had left.

"I started cutting down on red meat a few years ago—watching cholesterol—and I'm afraid I lost my taste for it. But I still like red wine." He said it apologetically, as if I might think less of him for the confession.

"That's okay. If I thought about what ranchers do to calves, I wouldn't eat red meat, either. And I'll reserve judgement on the red wine."

Curtis smiled and nodded, and there was a moment of embarrassing silence that I didn't know how to break.

"I'm glad you weren't tied up on your case tonight," he said finally. "What are you working on? Can you tell me about it?"

"Guy Scope's defense." That was the public story, and I could tell him that much.

"Do you really think he's innocent?"

"Yeah, I really do. I just don't believe he bashed his mother over the head and dumped her body in the swimming pool. But don't ask me who's guilty. I have no idea who did it."

"It sounds like a crazy thing to do," Curtis said, nodding. "Still, the paper this morning said that Guy was undergoing psychiatric evaluation."

"He's at Lake's Crossing Center now. And he is nuts, whether they say he can stand trial or not. In fact he is so nuts that I don't think he's capable of murdering his mother and then creating the story about a spaceman to cover it up. I have nothing to base that opinion on—my only contact with him was sitting next to him for two hours in a dark theater—but a lying mother-basher wasn't the way I sized him up."

"You trust your instincts, don't you?"

"That's how I stay alive," I said, and immediately

regretted it, because I didn't want to talk about the incident at the hunting lodge.

His brow furrowed again, but before he could ask a question, the waiter presented a bottle of wine for his inspection. By the time Curtis checked the label, and the waiter uncorked the wine, and Curtis tasted the wine, and the waiter poured for both of us, the moment had passed.

"What do you think?" was the question Curtis asked after I had taken a sip.

"I don't know what words you're supposed to use to describe wine. But it's fine. I could even learn to like it."

"Be careful. Some things that are acquired tastes—wine is one of them—are hard to get rid of." He smiled as he said it. I was starting to like his smile.

I didn't know how to respond to what he said, though, and there was another awkward silence.

"About Guy Scope," Curtis said. "What's your line of attack?"

"I'm not sure I have one. I'd like to find the sniper who shot at Gloria after the graduation ceremony. I wish I had one of your handy profiles to rely on." I smiled, so he'd know it wasn't a slam.

"A profile of a sniper? Unless you're talking serial sniper or mass murderer, I'm not certain there is one."

"No, I wouldn't think so. Besides, I'd bet this one was hired. So I'd have to have a profile on who was likely to hire a sniper to scare someone."

"Do you have a suspect?"

"I just can't get into that, I'm sorry." Another moment of silence. "But I do appreciate that you already gave me a profile of Tella—not that I suspect her—when you talked about entrepreneurs—although it doesn't fit either of her brothers."

"You're right." He shook his head thoughtfully. "It doesn't appear that either of them inherited the entrepreneurial gene. Or the sex drive that usually goes with it. At least in men." He added that quickly.

"What do you mean?"

"Well—I probably shouldn't have mentioned it—but most men who do what Ted Scope did, starting business after business, living on the edge, have a need for high-risk behavior in other areas, too. So they often have more than one woman in their lives."

I thought of the hunting lodge, the flushed toilet, and Tella's remark about wives being unwelcome.

"Would Ted Scope have had casual affairs or something longstanding, like a mistress?"

"I'd guess he had a mistress." Curtis was becoming uncomfortable, and I was sorry I had to pursue it.

"Would anyone have known who she was besides his buddies in the millionaires' club?"

"What's that?"

"Ted Scope and the Three Stooges—Warfield, Harding, and Zabriskie—own a hunting lodge in the Sierras, but they evidently use it for other sports. And I don't think they'd rat on Scope, even though it wouldn't hurt him now."

"Well—he probably had dinner with her somewhere. And there would probably be purchases, an accountant might be aware of her. Or someone who answered the phone at the office."

Chareese. Next time we talked, I had to get past her prepared press release.

"Why do you want to talk with the mistress? If there is one," Curtis added.

"When the wife was killed? Let's say I can't rule her out as a suspect."

"That does make more sense than saying the boy did it."

"Right."

We smiled at each other, and this time the awkward silence was broken by the waiter, who deposited our salads and went through the ground-pepper ritual. Curtis wanted some, I didn't.

"Another acquired taste," he said.

"Have you acquired a taste for Reno yet?" I asked. I had fortunately managed to remember that I wanted to find out more about him.

"I'm working on it. Reno's an attractive place to live—it has four seasons, with only a few days of excessive cold in the winter, and so far the summer hasn't been excessively hot. The desert to the east and the mountains to the west are both scenic wonders. And there's a satisfying intellectual and artistic community at the university."

"Did the chamber of commerce hire you? You could join the other poster boys welcoming tourists to the Reno airport."

"No." He laughed. "And I don't know any of the professors who posed for those ads. Although I'm certain they must have had good reasons to do it—beyond the obvious self-promotion."

"That's generous of you. What brought you here? And where did you come from?"

"I moved here from Southern California. As to what brought me here"—he frowned and hesitated before going on—"I'm afraid it's complicated."

"Does that mean you don't want to tell me?"

"No, of course not." Curtis looked me in the eye. He continued quietly. "My father died, my marriage fell apart, I turned forty, and I wanted very much to start over. The university was searching for someone in my area, and we seemed like a good fit."

"Do you think you'll stay?"

"Yes, I think so. I may even buy a pair of cowboy boots to symbolize my commitment to the area."

We smiled at each other through a silence that wasn't quite as awkward.

I was discovering why so many people eat on dates. Food is a great way to bridge the silences.

We talked a little more about Warfield, and the ethics of his grant to the business school, but the conversation didn't add much to what I knew. It also didn't change my opinion of Warfield.

When the check came, I was ready. I grabbed it while Curtis was reaching for his wallet.

"Do you really want to do that?" he asked.

"I really do. If I accept two dinners in one week, I'll feel indebted, and that will make me uncomfortable."

"Then *I* accept. I don't want you to feel uncomfortable."

I'd learned when I picked up checks with Sam that the waiter, salesperson, or whoever is handling the transaction has trouble putting the credit card slip in front of the right person. But this guy actually read the name on the card. I added a lot to the tip.

"It's still early," Curtis said as we were waiting for the elevator. "Would you like to catch a movie?"

"Not tonight. I'm tired, and I'm not sure I could concentrate on one." In truth, the last drop of adrenalin from the hunting lodge was finally draining away, and I could hardly keep my eyes open.

"Then I'll walk to your car."

"I didn't bring one. Home isn't that far."

"Will you accept a ride home?"

I would have refused, but I felt relief in my toes at the thought of a ride.

We got off the elevator at ground level and worked our way between twenty-one tables and roulette wheels to the back alley that separated the casino from the parking lot. I kept my head down, so that I wouldn't catch the eyes of anyone I knew, like Deke, who might ask why I wasn't taking care of business. I was going to get right back to it, and I didn't have to explain that.

Curtis had a maroon Volvo, parked on the first floor. I wondered what kind of parking god he knew personally, to find a space on the ground floor.

I gave him directions down Virginia, along Mill, and pointed out the corner where my house was. He turned and pulled up in front.

"Thanks for the ride," I said.

"Thanks for dinner. I hope we can do it again soon."

"Sure." Even as I was saying it, I had unfastened my seat belt and opened the car door. I didn't know if he wanted to kiss me, but I knew I wasn't ready to be kissed.

Curtis sat there until I was safely inside, then drove away. I was relieved that he hadn't tried to come to the door or anything, partly because I didn't want to be kissed and partly because it had suddenly hit me that if Larry the Lamb had someone watching me, whoever it was had just spotted Curtis, too. I didn't want to lead him into any kind of trouble.

The office was just as I left it. I picked up the phone and punched Tella's number, standing next to the desk. My chair still held Larry Agnotti's shadow.

"Just checking," I said when she answered.

"You're trusting. It's been more than a couple of hours."

"I was so trusting I went out for dinner."

"Anyone I know?"

Shit.

"Curtis Breckinridge."

"My mother would approve. I'm sure you make a lovely couple."

"Goddamn it, we just had dinner."

"It's all right, Freddie, really it is. And she would approve. Is there anything else you wanted? I'm working."

"One more thing. What's Chareese's last name?"

"Fraser. But if you're thinking of calling, her number isn't listed."

"Could you give it to me? I have some questions about incoming calls to the office, and I don't want to leave them until Monday."

Tella was silent, as if she had to think about it, but then I heard computer keys clicking. She gave me the number.

"Thanks," I said. "I'll call you in the morning."

"Get a good night's sleep." She said it dryly, as if it were code for "go to hell."

Gravity was attacking every cell in my body, urging me to lie down, but I punched out Chareese's number. I recognized the lilting hello.

"This is Freddie O'Neal. I need to talk with you," I said. "Away from the office. About Ted Scope, and a woman who might have called him a lot."

"Why should I tell you anything?" she asked.

"Because Ted and Gloria are both dead, and the answers might save Guy."

"All right. One o'clock tomorrow. Wingfield Park at the west tip of the island."

I was so tired I sat in the chair for a moment before I could think about heading for the bedroom. I got up because Butch was on the desk staring at me and Sundance was making sorrowful meows in the hall, lamenting his fate, to live with a woman who won't even open a can to feed him when he's starving.

I got the can open and into a dish. I even got to the bedroom and got my boots off. But I was asleep before I could turn out the lights and pull up the covers.

Chapter
10

RENO LIES AT the western end of Truckee Meadows, the flatland irrigated by the Truckee River, which runs through the middle of town on its way from Lake Tahoe in the mountains to Pyramid Lake in the desert. The Virginia Street bridge across the Truckee is the historical seed from which the settlement, then known as Lake's Crossing, grew. In 1868 somebody from the Central Pacific—I'd say Charles Crocker, who liked to name railroad stations, except he wasn't from Virginia—passed over Lake's Crossing in favor of Reno. So General Jesse Lee Reno, a Virginian who fought for the Union, died during the Civil War, and never came west, had the city named after him. Innkeeper Myron Lake's name survived on Lake Street, which is two blocks east of where it should be, and Lake's Crossing Center, where Guy Scope's psyche was being evaluated, which is several miles east, in Sparks, not Reno.

The only story I've heard about how the Truckee got its name could have come out of *Oh, Nevada*—Truckee was supposedly the name bestowed by frontiersmen on an Indian who ran the ferry across the river. Actually, with the river named after him, he may have gotten the last laugh.

Most of the condescending frontiersmen died in the mountains, and nobody remembers their names at all.

Even on the riverbanks, there wasn't a great variety of native flora—one of the early causes for friction between the Indians and the settlers was the invaders' nasty habit of clear-cutting vast stands of piñon trees, which they saw as useless, and thus depriving the Indians of the pine nuts that were staples in their diet. The deciduous trees in Wingfield Park—named after George Wingfield, a post World War II community leader—were all imports, every last locust and black walnut, along with the smooth green grass.

In the Sierras, the Truckee River is a clear, blue-white flow that dances whimsically over the rocks and down the gullies. In Wingfield Park, a couple of blocks west of the original Lake's Crossing, the brown water that flows sluggishly over the dam built to keep it under control, to curb its unfortunate habit of overflowing its banks when the snows melt, has a different, sadder character.

The park has tennis courts, which were full that Sunday afternoon as I walked past them toward the island. The grass was scattered with men and women in shorts, breathing the soft June air and waiting to play. A woman sat on a blanket in the sun, earphones on, eyes shut, as the Sheltie who had been sitting next to her decided to explore the next tree, in violation of the leash law and surely, sooner or later, in violation of the pooper-scooper law as well.

I reached the tip of the island right around one. I shared the area with an unshaven man in a greasy stocking cap and tattered overcoat who managed to look cold despite the high sun. We gave each other a lot of space. He stayed under a tree, I sat on the concrete embankment at the point, where the dark water eddied slowly as it forked.

I didn't see Chareese arrive. She suddenly settled next to

me on the grass, crosslegged, a sharp contrast to the greens and browns with her orange-and-white blouse, white skirt, and orange sandals. And her large gold hoop earrings.

"I don't think the boy did it, but I don't think she did it, either." The words came out with no preamble, a continuance of the telephone conversation the night before.

"Who is she?"

"Ted's friend. That's who you're asking me about, right?"

"Right. Tell me about her."

Chareese tugged at her skirt with long, slender fingers that ended in short, natural nails, until she was satisfied with the way it draped over her ankles. Her face had the same slender bones in both cheeks and jaw that marked her hands. Once through with her skirt, she turned her full attention to me, appraising me with large, dark eyes, still trying to decide how much to tell me.

"Her name is Karen Hackstaff. All I can tell you is that she works at the Mother Lode. I never met her and I don't know what she does there."

"But you talked to her on the phone."

"I did. For the year or so before he died, she'd call Ted maybe a couple of times a week at the office. When he was in the hospital, she called me every day for the word on his health. I promised I wouldn't tell, and now I'm breaking that promise, not because I think she did anything, but because I understand you have to follow up everything to help the boy."

"If she loved Ted Scope, why are you so sure she didn't kill his wife?"

"I just don't think she had the guts to get mad. All the time we talked on the phone, she never sounded like a woman who had the guts to get mad."

"Who else knew about her?"

"I don't know. Maybe nobody. I didn't talk, not to Tella or any of them." A cloud passed over the sun, and Chareese shivered in its shadow.

"That must have been tough. Tella trusts you, and so does Mike."

"Yeah. It was. But they all know I don't talk."

"What else, Chareese? What else don't you talk about?"

"If I knew anything that would help the boy, I'd tell you," she countered.

I thought about that. I searched for the right question.

"Do you know anybody who hated Gloria Scope—and had the guts to kill her?"

"That's the interesting thing, because a year ago I would have said Ted. And then he went and left her the business. I wonder sometimes if he didn't set it up that way, certain that if she controlled the company, somebody would get mad enough to take her out."

"If he hated her so much, why didn't he get a divorce?"

"Are you kidding?" Chareese shook her head in disbelief. "No way could he have raised enough cash to buy out her share of the corporation—not even if he gave her the house and everything else free and clear. We're not just talking simple community property here. Everybody thinks Gloria came into the marriage broke, because she was dealing twenty-one when Ted met her. But I happen to know that some of the start-up money was hers. What would that have been worth today? And how long could a couple of smart lawyers keep the two of them fighting over it?"

"Okay. Ted Scope thought he had to stay with Gloria until one of them died. Tella doesn't seem to be aware of her parents' marital problems, or at least she hasn't said anything to indicate that she is. So neither one talked much to her. But if Ted was setting Gloria up, he must have had someone in mind to do the job. Who would he have confided in?"

"I guess that brings you back to Karen Hackstaff, which was where we started out." Chareese stood up and started brushing grass from her skirt.

"Before you go—do you know anything about the spaceman? The one Guy said he saw in the backyard?"

"Guy was never in the office. I only know about things that happened in the office." She was almost swaying, poised for flight. Her eyes were focused somewhere else.

"Will you let me know if you think of something more that happened at the office that might help Guy?"

"I'll do that."

I watched her walk to the bridge and cross back toward the tennis courts along Arlington Street. I could have gotten more from her if I had known the right questions, I was certain of it. But she wasn't going to sit there while I fished, and she wasn't going to volunteer much. I imagined her as Larry the Lamb's agent. It was easier to see Chareese in that role than Beatriz. I considered breaching my promise to Larry and asking her flat out, and immediately reconsidered. I would have to find another way.

I was home again by two, and I checked in with Tella yet again.

"I'm here," she said. "I'll see you in the morning."

The telephone directory had a listed number for a Karen Hackstaff, with an address on Whitaker Drive, a street in a quiet neighborhood just west of the university that had been chopped into a pretty good half and a not-so-good half when Interstate 80 became a freeway. Karen Hackstaff lived in the good half. I drove over to see if she was home.

The block she lived on was an unlikely combination of a few old tract homes, unadorned rectangles built after World

War II that clung stubbornly to their foundations, and several newer architectural experiments in stucco and glass, some of which were too big for their lots. The decline of the front yard was documented by the decades. The newer the house, the less yard in sight.

The number I was looking for was painted on the curb in front of a collection of juniper trees that obscured the house from the street. The pathway through the shrubbery was created from carefully laid segments of broken concrete.

For a moment I thought I had stumbled onto an enchanted cottage. The rough-hewn wood that framed the two-story house was as dark as gingerbread. And the front porch that stretched to the right of the door was wide enough to be from an earlier century. A swing built for two, with a red-and-white striped seat, was gathering dust. The section of the house to the left of the door jutted forth to the edge of the porch. The large picture window would have a wonderful view of the juniper, but not much more, summer or winter.

I rang the bell and waited. I had my finger up there, ready to ring a second time, when the door opened.

"Yes?"

The woman who asked that question wasn't much older than Tella. She was wearing a yellow tank top and white shorts that barely covered the kind of body that adolescent males have wet dreams over. Chestnut hair curled around a heart-shaped face, free of makeup, with innocent eyes and full mouth, and fell all over her tanned shoulders. If it hadn't been for the fine lines forming at the corners of her eyes, the slight deepening of the shadows underneath, she could have passed for twenty.

If this was Karen Hackstaff, I'd bet Chareese was right. She didn't have the guts to kill Gloria Scope.

I didn't much want to talk to her, this woman who was Tella's father's girlfriend, and I wished I hadn't rung the bell.

"Karen Hackstaff?"

She nodded.

I fished a business card out of my pocket and handed it to her.

"I've been hired to help with Guy Scope's defense," I said. "Could I talk with you?"

"Do you have to?" The innocent eyes begged me to forget the whole thing and go away.

"I think so."

"Come in, then. But you can't stay too long—I'm expecting somebody soon."

The living room was sparsely furnished, as if the sofa and two chairs, all covered in a pink, blue, and beige swirl, had been bought for a smaller space. The desert landscape over the sofa, the only art, might have come from a garage sale. The junipers hid the house so well that a white torchère in the corner was lit, even though it was still a sunny afternoon outside.

Karen Hackstaff gestured toward the sofa. A magazine with a lot of colorful celebrity photographs lay open on the coffee table, close to one end of the couch. I sat at the other end. She took a chair, sitting like a little girl, with her knees close together and her hands clasping them tightly.

"I never met Guy, or his mother," she said.

"I didn't really think you had. But Ted Scope must have talked about his wife and children."

"Sometimes. Not a lot. How much do you know about my relationship with Ted?"

"I don't know anything about it. I'd like to hear whatever you want to tell me."

She shrugged her shoulders and shook her head, all in one motion, setting chestnut curls rippling.

"That's silly. I don't want to tell you anything. Ted never wanted anyone to know he was seeing me. I minded a little bit while he was alive, but now that he's dead, I'd just as soon not talk. I think Chareese was the only one who knew. Did Chareese send you?"

"Does it matter?" I didn't want to be the one answering questions here.

"I suppose not. If she did, she must have thought it was important."

I wasn't going to be drawn in.

"Is there anything about your relationship with Ted Scope that would help prove his son Guy isn't a murderer?"

"Probably not. I mean, what can I tell you anyway? If I say that Ted didn't love his wife, you probably won't believe me. You'll probably think he just wanted me to believe he didn't love his wife."

Karen Hackstaff was partly right. I would have thought that if Chareese hadn't said the same thing.

"She didn't love him, either," Karen continued. "But the money thing was so tangled they couldn't figure out how to split. Besides, they weren't hostile or anything, and they pretty much lived their own lives."

"I don't have trouble with that. Did Gloria know about you?"

"Maybe not by name. But she knew Ted was seeing somebody. You know," she said, looking at me for the first time, "if Ted hadn't already had one heart attack, I would have wondered if she killed him. That's why it's so strange, that she was the one who got killed."

Much as I liked Gloria, I couldn't leap in to defend her.

"But she was killed. And since Ted died last year, I think

we can safely assume that he didn't do it. Do you have any thoughts on who the murderer might be?"

"Tella." She said it firmly, a judgment made. "Even if Guy was the one who hit her, it was Tella who killed her. Tella made him do it."

"What did Ted say that makes you think so?"

"He told me that Tella hated her mother and wanted the company. He said that he was leaving it to Gloria, but he knew Tella wouldn't let her have it. Tella's clever, though— she won't be caught."

"Ted Scope said that?"

"More or less. Maybe not exactly that."

"What did he say exactly?"

"Stuff. I don't remember. He liked to talk about business, and I didn't listen to much of it. All he wanted me to do was nod, and I didn't have to listen to do that."

"Why didn't he just leave the company to Tella and the boys?"

Karen looked blank.

"I guess he didn't want to," she said.

"Right. I guess not." I did have trouble believing that all of Ted Scope's words had gone in one of Karen's ears and out the other, but she was certainly doing her best to convince me. "Did you know the three other men involved in the company—Warfield, Harding, and Zabriskie?"

"A little." She looked down and shifted in her chair.

"Did you spend weekends with Ted at the hunting lodge when the others were around?"

"What does that have to do with Guy killing his mother?"

"Somebody took a shot at Gloria, two days before she was murdered. I thought it might be someone with a hunting rifle."

"I wouldn't know about that. I never saw anyone hunt."

"What did you see?"

"I saw them play a lot of poker. That's all." She faced me on the last words. "And I'm afraid I don't have any more time to talk with you. I told you I was expecting someone. You'll have to leave."

I didn't argue with her. I got up from the sofa and walked to the door. She was right at my heels, so that when I turned on the threshold she couldn't get away.

"I believe you cared about Ted Scope," I said. "Even if he bored you when he talked about the company. And I can't believe you care so little what happens to his son. Call me when you want to talk."

I threaded my way through the junipers to the street without looking back.

I wanted to know who Karen Hackstaff was expecting, but I didn't want the Jeep to advertise my presence. I drove on down the block, turned around, and parked behind a beige van. About fifteen minutes later a black Range Rover pulled up in the space I had vacated.

The door opened, and I expected to see Tom Warfield get out of it. But Karen Hackstaff's visitor was George Harding. And Harding was the one member of the hunting lodge who admitted to owning and using a rifle.

Going back to ask more questions occurred to me. I didn't do it because I figured they would both be around, and confronting Harding in a tryst would only make him more hostile than he already was. I drove home instead, wondering if Deke could help me out on Karen Hackstaff.

The blinking light on my office answering machine reminded me that I still hadn't returned Ramona's call from the day before. This time the message was from Curtis Breckinridge, saying he wanted to see me again.

Shit.

What was I going to do with this nice man? I could imagine him offering Larry the Lamb a psychological profile of a mafioso. Rejects established authority in favor of private code, eagerly accepts unpleasant tasks in order to rise through the system, seeks out business situations in which competition is easily discouraged, prefers hands-on involvement. Have gun, will travel.

I could think about Curtis later. I called Ramona.

"I saw you on television," she said. "When the reporter was talking to the camera, you were in the background, going up the courthouse steps, for Guy Scope's hearing. Was Gloria Scope actually your client? I hope you didn't lose another client."

I didn't want to get angry with her. I really didn't want to get angry with her. Getting angry with my mother didn't do either one of us any good. I knew that, even as my face flushed and my scalp prickled. I took a deep breath and waited until my throat wasn't constricted before I answered.

"No, she wasn't my client. Guy Scope is. I've been hired to help with his defense."

"Well, thank God he's in jail, then, where nobody can get at him."

"Goddamn it, Ramona, that's enough." So much for good intentions. "I haven't made a career of losing clients. You hired me, and nothing happened to you."

"That's true, and I'm glad you reminded me. I was just so worried, and I knew you'd be upset if you'd been hired to protect Gloria and someone murdered her anyway."

"You're right. I would have been upset. I knew her, and I'm upset enough about that. But I wasn't hired to protect her. And I'm not protecting Guy Scope—I'm just working on his defense."

"Well, that's fine, dear. I'm glad you're working. I was

only concerned about you. And I know you would have called if you had realized that you were on television."

She was only concerned about me, and maybe Al as well.

"I would have, I swear," I told her.

That was a little much. She hesitated while she thought about it.

"I suppose if you're busy, you won't be up for a while. Especially if it's a long trial. We would like to see you, though, and the weather is lovely up here."

"It's lovely down here, too. I'll let you know when I have some time."

We said good-bye with as much goodwill as we could muster.

I still wanted to ask Deke about Karen Hackstaff. I would have waited for evening, and met him at the Mother Lode for dinner, but I wasn't up for another lecture about losing clients. I punched his number.

"Karen Hackstaff," I said when he answered. "Works at the Mother Lode, and a close friend of the late Ted Scope."

"Pretty thing," he said. "Smart, too. Deals roulette, swing shift, five-dollar table."

"Smart? She's smart?"

"Fooled you, did she?"

"How do you know she's smart?"

"Because dealing roulette requires some mathematical ability, and she wouldn't be on a heavy table, raking it in, if she didn't have something upstairs."

"What else do you know?"

"Nothing, but I'll ask for you. You protecting your client?"

"I'm doing my best, Deke. I'm doing my best."

"That's good, because somebody thought he saw you

having dinner here last night, upstairs in the Comstock Room, and it didn't look like business."

"Yeah, well, sometimes appearances are deceiving."

He accepted that, and I escaped from one more conversation with my self-esteem almost intact. Still, I was a little uncomfortable that Deke and Ramona seemed to have me covered. And they weren't really trying. A pro could do a lot better.

I called Tella, who assured me she was in for the night, even though it wasn't dark.

I decided that I was in, too. I played Tetris until I was hungry, then I had a pizza delivered for dinner. There were a couple of Clint Eastwood spaghetti Westerns on cable to get me through the evening, and I set the alarm to meet Tella in the morning.

Exhaustion knocked me out right after Lee Van Cleef shot Eastwood's hat to pieces. I slept until the alarm woke me.

Six-thirty came too early. When the alarm buzzed, I jolted upright, sending both Butch and Sundance flying. They stared at me unhappily from the carpet, not sure whether to get back up on the bed or go out. As I crawled out of bed toward the bathroom, first Butch and then Sundance found a nest in the disorder of the blankets and went back to sleep. I briefly considered tossing them into the yard.

My hands were shaking as I brushed my teeth and washed my face. The weekend hadn't been restorative. Nevertheless, I managed to be waiting at Tella's front door before Beatriz threw the coffee out.

Tella was impressed by my punctuality, if not by my appearance. I realized I was wearing the same shirt and jeans I had worn on Friday. Laundry was on my list, but it would have to wait a day or two.

I followed Tella on the by now familiar route. One more

time the guard let us into the parking lot, and I pulled the Jeep in next to the BMW.

The difference in the day first hit us both when we tried the front doors of the building, which were locked. Tella opened them, and went in.

The difference hit us harder when we realized the reception area was empty.

Chareese wasn't there.

Chapter
11

EVERY MONDAY MORNING, all over America, people fail to show up for work. Sometimes they oversleep, sometimes the kid is sick, sometimes the car won't start. Usually they show up in an hour or so with a simple explanation, and no one has bothered to sound an alarm in the meantime. Other employees fill in, and life goes on.

Usually.

"When's the last time Chareese was late?" I asked.

"Never," Tella answered. "She has never been late, not in four years."

She unlocked first the inside door and then the one to Chareese's cubicle.

"No messages on the machine," she added, leaning across the threshold.

She moved on to the open area, where two men and a woman were huddled around a computer terminal.

"Did Chareese call?"

All three murmured negatives without looking up.

Tella went back to the cubicle, picked up the phone, and punched out a number. After a moment she replaced the receiver, shaking her head.

"Should we call the police?" she asked.

"I don't think we could convince them to do anything quickly," I told her. "Unless you're talking about a child, they tend to think anybody can disappear for a day or so with no harm likely. And there haven't been any threats made against Chareese that I know of."

"Then you have to go over to her house," Tella said, in a tone that let me know she didn't expect an argument.

"Sorry. I can't leave you here without someone taking care of the door."

"It'll be locked. The only people who can get through will be long-time employees with passkeys, the ones who tend to work through the night when they get involved with a project."

I shook my head.

"We'll have to send someone else." I reached past her and picked up the phone. If I was lucky, Deke was home from the graveyard shift, but he hadn't gone to sleep yet. For once, I was lucky. He answered on the third ring. "Which would you rather do, check somebody's house to make sure she's alive or come to Scope Chips and answer phones while I check somebody's house?"

"Give me somebody's address," he said.

I asked Tella for the address and relayed it to Deke. I also described Chareese, just in case.

"I'll get back to you," he said.

"Who was that?" Tella asked.

"A friend. I don't suppose there's anyone else who can answer the phones while we're waiting."

"No. But the system isn't difficult. There's an intercom and a pager, and any phone can pick up any line. I'm sure you can handle it. And if you insist on staying, you might as well be useful."

While she was explaining how to use the intercom, two

people came in, expressed surprise at Chareese's absence, and were buzzed through.

"There's one more thing," I said when she had finished. She had been right, the phone system wasn't complicated. "How do I know who has clearance to go in?"

"Employees have ID cards. If you're in doubt, my intercom number is eleven." She pointed to the card that connected names and numbers. Hers was at the top.

"Got it. Now, if you don't mind, I'll see you safely to your office."

She did mind, but I had to make certain that no one had taken advantage of Chareese's absence and the single-minded absorption of the programmers to slip in.

"What about the mainframes?" I asked, pointing to the closed doors that protected them.

"One operator," she said.

"Check with him."

She did. He hadn't seen or heard anyone, and he'd been there since six.

I also insisted that she check the two empty offices, the one that belonged to Mike and the one that used to be Ted's. Nobody. And her office looked clean. She assured me that nothing had been touched since Friday, except that the cleaning crew had emptied the basket under the shredder and run a duster over the computer, something they did every Sunday.

I left her there and went back to Chareese's desk.

Nobody called for the first hour. Then there were two calls in a row from programmers, and each picked up when paged. I was starting to get edgy, but the next call was from Deke.

"Hell," he said. "You really are answering the phone."

"Did you find Chareese?"

"No. I didn't break into the condo, but nobody answered the bell, and the neighbors on either side didn't spot anything unusual. One pointed out to me that her car was gone. You got enough to talk to the police?"

"Well, I sort of have to talk to Matthews today about a rifle I dropped off on Saturday. I might mention Chareese as well."

"And just how did you happen to get a suspicious rifle?"

"He'll probably want to know that, too." When Deke didn't respond, I added, "Look, I'm sorry I didn't tell you I picked up a rifle at the hunting lodge on Saturday. I meant to, but I guess I forgot."

"I guess you better start remembering. You can try your story on me before you face Matthews. I'll be there in twenty minutes."

It took him twenty-five, but that wasn't bad time for an address on the other side of the city.

"So," he said, leaning on the counter, face and shoulders squeezed into the opening in the glass partition. The edge was cutting into the layer of fat that smoothed the transition from biceps to triceps. He had to be uncomfortable.

"The caretaker at the lodge took a shot at me, but he insisted that he meant to miss."

Deke scrunched his eyes and pinched his nose to let me know what he thought of that story.

"I couldn't have walked out of there with the gun if it had been used to hunt anything other than deer," I argued. "Warfield wouldn't pull that kind of bluff—but it doesn't cost me anything to see the hand."

"And this is what you're going to tell Detective Matthews?"

"The couple of times I've met him he's seemed okay. I

don't want to lie to him. Besides, I can't say I found the gun in a garbage can, and I can't think of a lie that would help."

"Good luck." He shook his head as if he thought bad luck was more likely.

"Thanks. I'll buzz you through the door. You'll have to watch this place until I get back. And you might as well answer the phone—the system isn't difficult."

"I do watch doors, I do not answer phones. Turn on the machine. I will listen, and if the voice on the speaker is either yours or Detective Matthews, I will pick it up."

"That's fine with me, but I have to let Tella know."

I hit the buzzer. When Deke opened the door, I slipped out of the cubicle so that he could maneuver his way in. It wasn't an easy fit.

I crossed the space to Tella's office, and her door popped open. She looked up from her terminal, startled, as if she had forgotten I was there.

"I'm going to the police station," I said. "Deke's watching the door, but he doesn't do phones. I'll get back as quickly as I can. And the phone hasn't been busy anyway."

"What about Chareese?" she asked.

"Car gone, no sign of her, he didn't break in. I'll try to talk Matthews into forcing entry."

"Good luck." Her tone was as gloomy as Deke's had been.

I smiled and nodded. As I stepped back, the door closed again behind me. I returned to the front, buzzed myself through the door to the reception area, and pushed open the glass front doors without pausing.

"See you," I called over my shoulder to Deke as the heavy doors swung shut.

I waved to the guard as he raised the crossarm to let the

Jeep out. I hoped he worked for Larry the Lamb, just in case Deke needed help before I got back.

The drive to the police station was maybe fifteen minutes, Kietzke to Second Street. Danny Sinclair was once again behind the desk, as glad to see me as ever.

"Matthews tried to call you," he said.

"I somehow sensed that. Tell him I'm here."

After a brief exchange on the intercom, Danny told me to follow the yellow line down the hall to Detectives. The colored lines on the floor marked the paths along which unescorted civilians could tread.

Matthews was waiting at the door. His full gray hair stood on end, as if he had been running his hands through it all morning. His tie was loose, and his white shirt was only about half tucked into his pants, straining over his beer belly. The sleeves were rolled past his beefy forearms to his elbows. Kind blue eyes were the outstanding features in a face that had lost the battle with gravity about the same time his waistline did.

"You didn't lie to me, did you, O'Neal?"

"What do you mean, sir?"

He motioned me into the room, and I followed him through a maze of desks, all overflowing with paper, most without people working at them, to the one with his nameplate. If anything, it was messier than the others. Matthews lowered his bulk into a solid chair behind it, and I was left with the flimsy one on the side.

"When we talked the day someone took a shot at Gloria Scope, you told me you just happened to be walking behind her when the incident occurred," he said, leaning back and lacing his fingers across his stomach. "Stranger things have coincided, so I didn't pursue the matter. Then the lady gets murdered, hit with a blunt object. A few days later you ask me to check out a rifle, even though it couldn't have been the murder weapon. Help me out here. Did you lose another client?"

Matthews had checked out more than the rifle. For once, I was grateful to Ramona. I had shot my wad of anger on that implication of incompetence already.

"No, sir. At no time was Gloria Scope my client, although she offered to hire me after the sniper incident you referred to. I am now employed to assist in Guy Scope's defense. In the course of that investigation, I came upon a rifle that I thought the police should run a ballistic check on. Of course, I brought it in at once."

"Glad to hear that," Matthews said, nodding. "I was beginning to think we should have a police backup on everyone who hired you as a bodyguard. You're a smart woman, but you're not a patient one. I can tell that by the way you sit on the edge of the chair, as if you're hoping I won't talk too long. A good bodyguard has patience."

"With due respect"—I knew he was baiting me, and I was doing my best—"I have only lost one client who hired me as a bodyguard. And my record working to exonerate persons unjustly accused has so far been unblemished."

"Very good, O'Neal. So where did you find this gun and why did you want it checked?"

"What did the ballistics test show?" I countered.

"Inclusive. And the prints were messed up, but I think you know that. So where did you find it?"

"It belongs to one of Tom Warfield's employees. I happened to see it while I was discussing the case with Mr. Warfield, and he encouraged me to borrow it."

"You think Warfield was the one who took a shot at her?" Matthews shook his head, squinting one eye, as if thinking that would make me embarrassingly naive. Or maybe thinking he believed my story would be embarrassingly naive.

"I think it's possible, if unlikely."

"But you do think that whoever took a shot at her wasn't Guy Scope, and you could try to link the attempt on her life to her actual murder."

"Yes."

He pulled on his chin while he thought.

"It's not a bad approach. Better than the spaceman defense, even if the kid is as crazy as a shithouse rat."

"Yes, sir. Is 'crazy as a shithouse rat' your professional opinion?"

"No. I do not express professional opinions on whether a defendant is legally sane. As a keen observer of human behavior, however, I would describe him as psychologically challenged. How's that?"

"Fine. Thank you."

Matthews leaned forward and started to lift himself from his seat.

"And there's one more thing." I spat it out so fast that he fell backward, rocking the chair. "The receptionist from Scope Chips didn't show up for work this morning. I'd like to file a missing persons report, and I'd like you to act on it immediately, circulating her description."

"Of course you already tried her home." This time he squinted both eyes. "Tell me, O'Neal, where you think she is and why you think she's missing."

"If I knew where, I'd be there. As for why—" I hesitated. Matthews waited. "I think it's connected to the murder, but I'm not certain how."

He opened the bottom drawer of his desk, riffled through some files, and pulled out a form. There wasn't a bare space on the desk, so he slapped it on top of the stack of papers in front of me.

"Fill it out and I'll do what I can. I can't promise anything."

He got up and walked away. I realized as I scanned the questions that I wasn't the best source of information where Chareese Fraser was concerned. I wrote down what I knew, then looked around for Matthews. He was standing across the room, cup of coffee in hand, chatting with another bulky guy in shirtsleeves. I stood up, and he made his way back.

"Keep in touch," he said, taking the form.

I followed the yellow line back to the front desk. I was spared saying good-bye to Danny Sinclair, who was on the phone.

I had planned to head straight back to Scope Chips, but as I pulled out of the parking lot, I thought about Deke saying that he had only checked with neighbors, he hadn't gone into the house. Probably she wasn't inside, since one neighbor had said her car was gone, but I needed to make sure.

Chareese's address was in a quiet district just across the Truckee from Reno High. I took Second Street to Keystone Avenue and looked for the number. It was one of a collection of wood frame buildings, slate blue with white trim. The grounds were bright green, dotted with beds of purple and gold pansies and orange marigolds. Scope Chips had apparently been paying Chareese well.

I parked in a space marked Visitor and walked up the stairs to the unit labeled D. I didn't expect an answer, but I rang the bell anyway. I even rang it a second time. I tried the doorknob, but the deadbolt was locked. Then I checked for another way to get in.

The condo sported a sundeck, with a railing that began

about ten feet from the stairway. The white ornamental ledge between looked solid enough to support my weight, although it was six inches wide at best. I placed the ball of one foot on it and tested. It would work. When neither my eyes nor my ears picked up a trace of neighbors or other watchdogs, I began inching my way toward the deck, holding on to the siding with my fingertips. The ledge was giving just enough to make me nervous. I hoped nothing would crack.

I didn't realize I'd been holding my breath until my right hand grasped the railing. I swung myself over and onto the deck. Chareese had decorated it with a half dozen potted plants and a small table with two wrought-iron chairs.

The sliding glass door had the kind of mechanism that latches it firmly to a metal frame. I would have had trouble getting it open, but somebody had already jimmied it. There were silver gashes, maybe from a crowbar, on the black steel. I used one finger at the top and one at the bottom of the handle to push it back. I didn't want to mess up prints, although I would have bet against there being any to mess up.

The living room furniture was the kind that looks as if it's composed entirely of cushions, in this case tan with a black design that may have been an abstract leaf or vine. The coffee table and the television stand were both some kind of dark wood. A *TV Guide* was open on the rug next to one of the cushions.

An oil painting of black figures encircling an extravagantly large orange-and-yellow butterfly took up one wall. Two others walls had bright hangings that were either African or inspired by African culture.

I moved on through the dining room—nothing on the table—to the short hall and the bedroom.

The bed was made, the black-and-white bedspread pulled smooth, the matching pillows tossed carefully against the black rattan headboard. Nothing looked out of place, no signs of a struggle. The answering machine on the night-stand showed one message. I knew Tella hadn't left one, so I hit the Playback button. Just a hangup and dial tone— Tella after all. I glanced in the closet, but I wouldn't have known if anything was missing.

The bathroom was right next to the bedroom. It hadn't been scrubbed—there were dried water spots and a couple of black hairs on the counter next to the basin—but it was still cleaner than mine. I felt the bristles on the toothbrush. They were too dry to have been used that morning. Chareese probably hadn't slept in the condo.

I went back to the bedroom closet. I wouldn't have known if something was missing, but I could check to see if something was there—the orange-and-white outfit Cha-reese had been wearing when I met her in the park. No sign of it hanging, or in the laundry hamper.

The only other room was the kitchen. I hadn't expected to find anything there, but I was wrong. Someone had left one of the drawers ajar. I hooked a finger on the edge to pull it open. Chareese hadn't had a desk, or any obvious place to store papers. This drawer seemed to be it. Paid bills and receipts—the kind of mess that has to be straightened out every year for income tax records—had been tossed like a salad. I used the palm of my hand to push the drawer back the way I had found it.

The kitchen counter was clear except for one heavy mug with a trace of dried coffee in the bottom.

I almost missed the spot of dried blood on the linoleum. It blended too well with the dark brown diamonds in the pattern. I didn't think it was Chareese's—I was figuring she hadn't been back since meeting me the day before. Somebody might have stuck a hand in the knife drawer by mistake. Or the crowbar used to jimmy the door to the deck might have slipped. Either way, there was evidence somebody had been inside.

There was one other thing I could do before returning to Scope Chips. I grabbed a handful of toilet paper from the bathroom, picked up the telephone receiver next to the bed, and punched the Scope Chips number.

I listened through the message and waited for the beep.

"Deke? You gotta pick up."

The machine clicked off as he lifted the receiver.

"What's happening?" he asked.

"I want to look around just a little for Chareese's car. Would you ask Tella what she drives?"

"How do I do that?"

"Just hit the button marked Page—it's the bottom left-hand one—and ask Tella to pick up the phone."

There was a pause while he found the right button. I heard him talking, then Tella was on the line.

"Chareese drives a white Nissan," she said when I explained what I wanted. "I don't know the model or year. Are the police going to do anything?"

"Not soon enough."

"How do you know where to look?"

"I don't. But I wanted to know what I was looking for. I'll tell you more when I get back."

"And when will that be?" Deke asked.

"Soon. Half an hour."

I considered leaving the condo the way I had entered— over the deck rail and along the ledge, which was what the first intruder had to have done—because I would otherwise have to leave the front door open. But I decided it wouldn't be open for long. Matthews had wanted me to keep in touch. A phone call once I got to Scope Chips should convince him to put a police seal on it.

I flipped the deadbolt, turned the knob, and then shut the door behind me with the toilet paper still shielding my hand. On the way back to the Jeep, I dropped the wadded-up paper in a trash can.

Second Avenue took me to Arlington, and I slowed to a crawl as I neared Wingfield Park, looking for a white Nissan.

Androgynous groups of twos and threes wearing red jackets and blue pants and carrying shiny brass trumpets, trombones, and saxophones were trotting along the sidewalk. One of the signs of summer in Reno—the noon band concerts in the park.

No Nissan on Arlington. I drove down Court, came back on Liberty. I was beginning to think that every third car for blocks was white, not one a Nissan, when I spotted a parked white car with a dark woman sitting in the driver's seat on Rainbow Street right next to the Episcopal church. I had to make a U-turn to get back to it. I double-parked the Jeep and got out. The woman didn't move.

From across the Truckee I heard the opening notes of "Strike Up the Band," a sound designed to bring cheer to brown-bagging office workers nostalgic for the days when the summer was one long picnic.

I saw that the car door was locked, and I didn't bother to rap on the window. I had already recognized the orange-and-white blouse, and the large, dark eyes that were focused on wherever it is that parallel lines meet.

Chapter

12

I'VE NEVER BEEN able to list neatly the reasons why I became a private investigator. Curtis Breckinridge and my college psychology instructor would both point out that it was a natural choice, since I fit the profile. I was a trapezoidal peg in a trapezoidal hole. My high school friend Kenny Urrutia would argue that the choice came from a need for redemption, a need to right wrongs as penance for my own childhood sins, both real and imagined. Ramona probably saw it as an enduring rebellion against her wish that I get married and have children.

Whatever pieces the analytic puzzle contained, the ability to cope calmly and professionally with the inert flesh of someone who had been vibrant the day before was missing. For a moment I didn't know how to deal with Chareese Fraser's dead body.

I knew I had to get hold of Matthews, but that meant leaving her there. It didn't matter that she had been alone in the car for almost twenty-four hours. I wanted to stand watch beside her, protecting her in death, when I hadn't protected her in life. I hadn't even realized she needed protection.

I don't know how long I would have stayed frozen. The

sound of an automobile horn, blaring discordantly above the faraway band, brought me to attention.

"Move your damn car!" a man's voice shouted.

I could have shouted back, but I took a few steps toward him so that my tone would be close to normal.

"I'd rather wait until the police get here. Would you mind calling them? This woman is dead."

For once in my life the anger came out as strength. A pale face behind the windshield nodded, then backed the green Chrysler up and maneuvered it carefully around my Jeep.

The black-and-white arrived some indeterminate time later. I was still standing by the door to the Nissan. The band had moved on to "Stars and Stripes Forever."

I explained as much as I could. One of the men called Matthews as well as the medical examiner. The other officer asked me to move the Jeep. This time I agreed. When I turned the key in the ignition, I realized my hands were shaking. I pulled forward about half a block, clearing the dark church, then left it double-parked again.

Matthews got there first.

"I thought you didn't know where to look," he said.

"I changed my mind."

"What changed it?"

"I drove by her condo, discovered that the door to the sundeck was open, and went in through the open door to see if I could determine how long she had been missing." I paused to see if that would elicit more than a raised eyebrow. It didn't. "When it appeared that she hadn't been home since yesterday, I decided to look for her car near the park. Lots of people come to the park on Sunday."

He shook his head. "Not good enough. More."

Another car drove up, followed by an ambulance. The man in the car exchanged a greeting with Matthews. Finally the door to the Nissan was opened. Chareese stayed rigid as the man touched her body.

"Why the park?" Matthews asked, still watching the activity around the car.

"If I knew who did this, I would tell you," I said. "If I even had a lead on who did this, I would give it to you. But what I really want to do, right after somebody says something about how she died, is get in touch with someone who cared about her."

"Bullet hole in the base of the skull," the man leaning inside the Nissan called out. "No exit wound. She probably died instantly, sometime yesterday, here in the car. Okay if we take her away?"

"Do it," Matthews said, just loudly enough for the words to carry. Then he turned back to me. "You going to Scope Chips?"

"Yeah."

"Wait for me there."

"I will. And tell whoever goes to the condo that the spot of blood on the kitchen floor isn't mine."

He nodded, then returned his attention to the Nissan.

I watched as Chareese was eased out of the car. The two men in paramedic scrubs couldn't straighten her body out to place it on the stretcher. One took her shoulders and one took her knees as if she were a mannequin, and they lifted her into the ambulance. I caught a glimpse of her back, rust-colored from dried blood.

That was enough. I said good-bye to Matthews and walked to the Jeep. My hands were still shaking, but I could make it to Scope Chips.

I drove slowly, trying to paint Chareese's death onto the same canvas that already held Gloria's. Chareese had sent me to Karen Hackstaff, presumably to help clear Guy, but

Karen Hackstaff had in fact tried to implicate Tella, which wouldn't clear Guy at all. So who would want Chareese dead? Tella? Karen Hackstaff? How about George Harding, who was apparently Hackstaff's new friend?

And who had known about the meeting?

Tella was the only person who knew I wanted to talk with Chareese. Unless one of our phone lines had been tapped. Or Larry the Lamb had left a bug in my desk. I suddenly felt very tired, when I realized that I hadn't thought of that before.

At least Guy Scope couldn't have committed this murder. Not that the same person had necessarily done both. But it helped his case, that he was still under evaluation. And if Tella could prove she hadn't left the house—if Beatriz could vouch for her—she was in the clear. I wondered if Mike had an alibi for the day before. Or if Larry the Lamb had one. A bullet hole in the base of the skull had echoes of the Mob.

The guard at Scope Chips raised the crossarm and waved me through without hesitating. I hoped he had buzzed Tella when he saw me coming. The alternative—that security was not as tight as I had been led to believe—was the next thing I would have to worry about.

I parked next to the teal BMW and pushed open the glass doors.

"That," Deke said, "was the longest half hour in history."

"Can it. Chareese Fraser was murdered. Shot right after I talked to her yesterday."

"Shit."

"Matthews will be along. I gotta talk to Tella first."

Deke hit the buzzer for the inner door.

The three programmers who had been there hours before

were eating sandwiches at their desks. Four others were working silently by themselves.

Tella's door popped open as I approached. I still found that unnerving.

I sat heavily in one of the chairs, searching for words.

"You found her," Tella said.

"I'm afraid I did."

Tella hit a couple of keys and turned off her computer. That, even more than the pallor of her face, let me know how upset she was.

"What happened?" she asked.

"Somebody got upset because she talked to me. Shot her in the head."

"Oh, God."

"Who do we notify?"

"I don't know." Tella seemed stunned at the thought. Then she started to laugh. "I don't know. Isn't that hilarious? A woman works in the same building with me for four years, and she is shot in the head, and I have no idea who her family is, who her friends are, or what relationships she had when she walked out the door."

"No," I said. "It isn't funny at all."

She quieted down after that.

"What about the police?"

"Matthews will be over a little later."

She took a deep breath. "Matthews. That's the same man. He'll have to let Guy come home."

"That's not the way it works. In the first place, he may not think the same person committed both murders. In the second place, the district attorney brought the charges, and the district attorney would have to drop them. Not necessarily a foregone conclusion."

"Oh, God," she said again. "What am I going to do?"

The last question was directed at the wall, somewhere above my right shoulder.

"First, you're going to pull yourself together. I can't deal with a hysterical woman."

That was better than a slap in the face. She sat bolt upright and turned to face me.

"Then you're going to think about whether there's anything you ought to tell me before Matthews gets here," I said. "Like whether you left the house yesterday, and where your brother Mike was."

"I was there all day. If you're asking for an alibi, though, I'm not sure that Beatriz could guarantee my whereabouts for the whole time. I could have slipped out quietly. I didn't, however. As far as Mike is concerned, you'll have to ask him. I didn't see him."

"Is he here?"

She picked up the phone and hit two digits, waited a moment, and shook her head.

"Try the house," I suggested.

She punched out a longer sequence of numbers.

"Beatriz, is Mike there?" Tella paused for the answer. "If you see him, please ask him to call me." She hung up the phone. "Beatriz says he left about an hour ago. She thought he was coming here."

"Do you have any idea where else he could have gone?"

She shook her head again. She huddled deeper into her chair, arms crossed, as if she were hugging herself.

"Can you tell me what's happening?" she asked.

"No. I wish I knew."

"Detective Matthews is here." Deke's voice boomed through the paging system, as if his mouth was right against the microphone. "I have buzzed him right on in."

Tella got up and walked around the desk to the door.

"Just making sure he doesn't detour," she said in answer to my unasked question.

She ushered Matthews in a moment later.

"I got nothing new for you, O'Neal," he said, taking the other visitor's chair. "You got anything new for me?"

"Not a thing. If you don't mind, I'll relieve Deke on the phones."

Tella looked as if she might mind. But when neither of them objected, I left.

The door to the cubicle was open. Deke didn't quite overflow the space, but closing the door would have been tight.

"Do you want to leave?" I asked. "I know you have to sleep sometime."

"Not right now I don't. With everything happening, I may not sleep before Friday. You said this woman was shot right after she talked to you yesterday. You called me yesterday to ask about Karen Hackstaff. I suspect there is a connection. And you were moving so fast this morning that I couldn't tell you I made a discreet inquiry about Karen Hackstaff. The word is she might have some nasty friends."

"What kind of nasty?"

"The kind you call on if you want someone's kneecaps hurt. That may or may not be the Mob. My informant wasn't specific."

"Okay. Are you willing to hold down the fort here while I do one more thing?"

Deke shut his eyes and dropped his head. "I just got sleepy." He opened his eyes again. "I'll be here. But this thing better not produce another dead body."

"Just something I have to find out," I said. "If Matthews wants me, tell him I'll be back."

"Hurry. He may not like finding out you're gone."

I sprinted to the Jeep and waved to the parking lot guard. He waved back and raised the crossarm. Lax security. I was glad both Deke and Matthews were there.

I drove home as quickly as I could without breaking the speed limit or otherwise drawing attention to myself.

I walked into my office and looked around. If I were planting a bug, where in all this disorder would I put it?

The obvious place was in or near the phone. It was an all-in-one plastic job, and while I could have shoved a screwdriver into one of the cracks to check the insides, I couldn't find the scratchmarks that anyone messing with it would have left. The layer of dust on the answering machine was undisturbed except for the shiny spots on Playback and Rewind.

The next obvious place was the lamp. But here again, the dust hadn't been disturbed. I was partly annoyed at myself for disgustingly bad housekeeping, partly congratulating myself that something good had come out of it. I turned to the desk itself. I straightened up papers so I could see the surface, then felt down the sides and looked underneath. I pulled out the long, narrow center drawer, dumped my random collection of working and nonworking pens, paper clips, staples, and so on, onto the carpet. Nothing in or behind the drawer.

I pulled out the top right-hand drawer, the one underneath the answering machine. Something small and metallic was suctioned to the bottom side of the desktop.

"Call me, Larry!" I shouted into the hole where the drawer had been. Then I pulled the bug loose, carried it out to the front porch, and stomped it hard with my boot. I stomped the pieces until I was certain it was destroyed.

I went back to my desk and sat down in the chair. Sundance was poking at the litter from the center drawer, batting one of the pens. I picked him up and hugged him. He struggled loose, but then he decided to stay, curling up into a cheerful orange ball.

Butch hopped onto the desk and scattered the papers I had just stacked, annoyed that I was petting his friend and rival. He thomped his tail and glared for a moment, then flopped over on his side to join whatever was going on.

I waited twenty minutes before the phone rang.

"I understand you wanted to talk to me, Miss O'Neal."

The voice was the smooth, gentle baritone I remembered from the one terrifying conversation I had had with him.

"Yes, sir. Thank you for getting back to me so quickly." I paused long enough to know that the ball was still in my court. "Excuse me for asking this, sir, but do you know anything about a hit on one Chareese Fraser?"

"I knew she met with you. This is the first I've heard about a hit. I wouldn't have ordered it, and I'm not happy about it. Miss Fraser worked for me. You might have suspected that."

"Yes, sir, I did. I hoped you weren't involved with her death, but I felt I had to ask."

"Anything else?"

"Yes, sir. It has also occurred to me that Karen Hackstaff might have some connection with your organization."

"Scope's mistress? The bimbo from the casino? She's strictly an amateur, although I've heard she plays rough. She isn't one of mine."

"And Beatriz?"

"You seem to have concluded that I like to work with women, and you're right. I find that women in this line of work tend to be both smarter than men and less likely to draw attention to themselves. On the rare occasions when brute force is necessary, I can always give them a backup."

The tone of his voice discouraged a follow-up question.

"Okay. Thanks. And I'll think about who else knew I was meeting Chareese."

"It might help you to know that there is an internal tap on the phone line at the Scopes residence. My operative suggests that Mike Scope is keeping track of what goes on, despite his apparent absentmindedness."

"Thanks for the information. I'll talk to him." I was afraid he was going to hang up, so I added quickly, "Is there a way I can get in touch with you?"

"I believe you destroyed the communication channel I had left for you. You can leave a message for me on Internet, however." He gave me an E-mail address.

The marvelous quality of an address on the information superhighway is that everyone can use it, and no one knows where it is.

"And don't forget, Miss O'Neal, that whatever else you're doing, I'm holding you responsible for my daughter's safety."

He hung up before I could ask anything more.

I drove back to Scope Chips and was waved through again. This time the guard looked relieved, as if someone had chewed him out for letting me escape.

Deke glowered as I walked through the door.

"How many dead bodies?"

"None. And I'm sorry I took so long. I moved as fast as I could. Is Matthews still here?"

"Left a few minutes ago. He didn't look happy when I told him I didn't know where you were. I assured him you would call." He paused to let that sink in. "Miss Scope is staying in her office under protest. And I am ready for bed. The excitement faded while I sat."

"Thank you for staying. I owe you. I'll collect Tella, and we can all get out of here. Matthews can wait till later."

"I hope he agrees."

Deke hit the buzzer to let me through the door. Tella had, in fact, left her office. She was sitting, alone, in the maze of desks.

"I sent everyone home," she said. "I had to. I couldn't ask people to keep working now."

"I'm sorry. I know meeting the June thirtieth deadline is important to you. Can you give everyone a day or two off and still make it?"

She shook her head. One hand came up and covered her eyes.

"I don't think so. I think I've just lost the company. Chareese is dead, I'm forced to confront the fact that I'm a self-centered idiot with no life but my work, and now I'm going to lose the company."

"Let me drive you home. You can leave your car here for the moment."

"I don't think you need to worry about me any longer. If this was designed to make me quit, I quit. I am not a threat to anyone who wants the company. If I was ever in any danger, it is over. And I can drive myself home."

With that, she squared her shoulders and stood. She still had the white face of a terrorized child.

"I'll drive you," I said calmly. "There's something I have to check."

"What?"

"Your brother Mike's room."

"Mike didn't have anything to do with this."

"Then where is he?"

Tella wavered for a moment, then reset her shoulders.

"All right. Let's go. Better you than Matthews." She

walked to the cubicle and paused in the doorway. "I'll be locking the building now, Mr. Adams. Thank you for your help. You can either include your bill with Freddie's or send a separate invoice."

"One way or the other, you're welcome." Deke had to slide out from behind the desk before he could stand up. "Call me, soon," he added for my benefit.

The three of us moved out to the parking lot together. Tella locked the door behind us.

"What about the guard at the gate?" I asked.

"He'll stay. There's also one computer operator inside. I offered them both double time."

Deke drove out and turned south. The crossarm stayed up until we followed in my Jeep. We turned north, then west on Plumb Lane. Neither of us felt much like talking.

There were no cars in the gravel parking area as we approached the castle. I stopped the Jeep just beyond the front door. Tella had leaned against the passenger window the whole trip. She got out and moved to the porch, then paused to disarm the security system.

I followed her into the central turret, across the Oriental rug, and up the stairs.

"What are you looking for?" she asked when we reached the second-story hall.

"Somebody had to know I was meeting Chareese," I said. "I'm looking for evidence that Mike was tapping phone calls."

She turned to face me. "I hate going into his room when he isn't here. We've always respected each other's privacy."

"Better me than Matthews," I said. "And there might not be anything to it."

Tella opened the door to Mike's bedroom.

There was a small, unmade bed against the right hand

wall. The computer workstation dominated the wall to our left. And a table under the windows held something else.

"What is it?"

"I'm not sure." She walked over and inspected the machine. "It's some kind of laser equipment."

I walked over to join her. The table held a long, pointed black tube aimed at a couple of dark squares.

"Can you turn it on and see what it does?"

She flipped a switch on a black box next to the tube.

A ruby light shot from the point, went through one square, and bounced off the other, landing on still a third.

While I was staring, puzzled, Tella went stiff. I followed her gaze out the window to the backyard.

The three-dimensional image of Ted Scope danced on the swimming pool below.

Chapter

13

"TED SCOPE'S GHOST," I said. "That explains part of Guy's story. What causes the effect?"

"It's a hologram. Mike had to have created it—that's what the ruby laser is for, to create the picture on specially treated film. The image must be imbedded in the pool cover. Mike could see it, Guy could see it, and our mother could see it. But the first-floor bedrooms are at the wrong angle, so I couldn't see it. You have to look at a hologram from the right angle, with the right light source."

Neither of us was ready to move. We stood side by side at the window, fascinated by the pale, eerie form.

"Would Beatriz have known about it?"

"We can ask. She couldn't have seen it from her bedroom, but she might have noticed it when she was cleaning one of the upstairs baths. It depends on angle and light."

Tella was starting to shiver. I hoped she wasn't going into shock.

"Now it's lit by the sun." I kept my voice low. "How could it be seen at night? Is the moon enough?"

"A full moon would be. And one of the backyard spotlights is focused on the pool." That was as far as she could go in her head. "What's going on?" she cried.

"I don't know. Although I suspect that your brother Mike is part of whatever it is. Let's talk somewhere else."

Even saying that, I wondered how much of the house was bugged. I was feeling edgy, and I didn't want to stay in Mike's room long enough to search.

"The library," Tella said. "We could sit in the library. I'll ask Beatriz to bring us tea. We can wait for Mike to come home, and then we can ask him about the hologram."

I could hear how desperately she wanted something to be normal.

"That's a good idea. Let's have tea."

I hoped waiting for Mike was a good idea.

I followed Tella back down the stairs and along the hall to the kitchen. I had decided not to let her out of my sight until I knew where Mike was.

Beatriz was alone in the kitchen. She nodded in response to Tella's request for tea.

The library was in the other wing. I was starting to know my way around. Despite the bright day, the library was cool. Tella turned on the gas log.

"All right," I said, sitting on the couch at the right side of the fireplace and wishing I believed that tea would improve the situation. "Let's try to put this together. Guy thought the hologram was his father's ghost, when he said he had seen it, and it wouldn't talk to Gloria. Would that have been part of some show Gloria was planning?"

"I think so. I don't know what it was going to be, but seeing the hologram—and remembering her performance at *Oh, Nevada*—I think she may have been planning something."

"With Mike," I said.

Tella nodded and moved to the left-hand couch. "I just don't understand why he didn't tell me."

I jumped right past that one. I didn't have the answer.

"Did you know Mike was involved in holography?"

"I didn't know he had the equipment. He became fascinated with it when our father had some holographic key chains made up a few years ago, as promotional giveaways for Scope Chips. We both insisted on having the technology explained. And you probably didn't notice—I forgot to point it out to you—but there are two holograms on the walls of his room. One is a lion that roars if you get too close to it."

"No. I didn't notice." I wondered if someone got so close to Mike that he had to roar. "Could there be a second hologram in the backyard? One of a spaceman?"

"In theory, I suppose. But there would have to be some kind of surface for it to be reflected against. And there are too many plants for one of the walls to work." She was silent for a moment, watching the low blue flame from the gas log. "It's also possible that Guy was just confused. Ghosts, spacemen, who knows."

"The ghost was real. I'm betting the spaceman is, too. And that it had something to do with a surprise that Gloria was planning, with Mike's help."

"Do you think Mike murdered her?"

"I don't know. I hope not. I told you. I'm just trying to figure this out."

Beatriz was placing a tray on the table before I heard her enter the room. There was a plate of blueberry muffins nestled between the teapot and the cups, and I remembered that I hadn't eaten all day. I wasn't very hungry, but I could handle a blueberry muffin.

I held up my hand to stop Beatriz from leaving the room.

"If you know something that will help, this is the time to tell us."

Tella looked at her and nodded.

"I know your brother Mike is unhappy," Beatriz said. "He tapes all the phone calls. And I knew he put the image of his father in the swimming pool." She turned to me. "You want me to say someone is a murderer, anyone is a murderer, you don't care who. But I care. I have lived with these children, loved them, and pitied them when their parents ignored them. You are a detective. If you want this solved, you solve it yourself. Don't ask me. You want to talk to Mike, he just drove up. I'll tell him you're having tea."

"Thank you, Beatriz. Please ask him to join us," Tella said. She waited until Beatriz left before adding, "I'm sorry. I don't know why she was rude to you."

"She was rude because she doesn't like the way this is going to work out. However it works out."

"What do you want in your tea?"

"Straight is fine. Thanks."

Tella poured two cups and handed me one. She added lemon to her own. Neither of us touched the blueberry muffins. I wasn't hungry after all.

"Maybe I ought to look for Mike," Tella said. "See what's keeping him."

"No. We'll wait here."

We had to wait too long, and I was wondering if I'd made a mistake in saying we should stay put, when we heard heavy footsteps in the hall. Too heavy, too spaced to be Mike's. I was also wondering if I should have brought a gun. But it was too late for that.

The second hologram appeared in the doorway.

Ted Scope's three-dimensional face smiled at us from a globular helmet. The body was Mike's—dressed in a suit and tie, ending in platform boots.

"You wanted to talk to Mike. Talk to me instead."

The voice was muffled, little more than a whisper.

"Oh, no, Mike," Tella said. Her eyes filled and over-flowed. She didn't seem to notice. "Don't do this. Please."

"I am not Mike. I am Ted Scope. I am your father. And I am in charge. You will do what I tell you to do, all of you."

"Sit down, Mike, have some tea." Tella poured another cup and held it out. "Tell me what happened."

"I am Ted Scope. I run the company. My wife Gloria wouldn't listen when I told her that. She said it was her company. But it is mine. I designed the chips—everyone knows that. I wrote the code that made them work. It is my company. You work for me."

He stayed in the doorway, ignoring Tella's offer.

I put my cup down. Under normal circumstances, I could take the kid in hand-to-hand combat. But I wasn't certain what he might do. Reinforcements seemed like the best way to avoid a fight. I leaned back and thought about slipping from the couch, easing my way toward the phone. It was on the other side of the room, though. No way to get to it without drawing his attention.

"We've talked about this, Mike," Tella said patiently. "We work together. No one works for anyone. I know you designed the chips. The company would be nothing without you. Sit down. Take off the helmet. Please."

"I am Ted Scope. And I brought someone with me who can prove it."

He clomped a couple of steps into the room, clearing the doorway.

Karen Hackstaff stood in his place. She was wearing the kind of slim skirt and full jacket that Tella liked, in a soft, rich ivory color a hundred and eighty degrees from what I had seen her in the day before.

"Tell them," Mike ordered.

"Of course, Ted," Karen said smoothly. "I'll tell them you're Ted Scope. Who would know if I don't?"

"Who are you?" Tella gasped.

"You don't know? I've been Ted's girlfriend for years, lots of people know that. Your friend here knew that. I guess his daughter just got left out of the circle." Karen smiled. It was as nasty a smile as I've ever seen in my life. "As of an hour ago, I'm his wife."

"This is Karen Hackstaff," I said, cutting in before Tella could say anything.

"Now Karen Scope."

I ignored her and continued. "She was Ted Scope's girlfriend. I found out yesterday. I think Chareese was killed because she told me."

"Chareese didn't want to work for me any longer," the voice from the helmet said. "I was sorry to lose her."

The image of Ted Scope's smiling face belied the words.

"This won't work," Tella said. She placed the teacup on the tray and touched the area beneath her eyes carefully, making sure it was dry. "Whatever you're planning. Even if you kill me, and even if no one discovers it, the outside members of the board will never agree to let Mike run the company."

"I'm certain that once the board members understand that Ted Scope is back, they won't have any problem with who runs the company," Karen said.

"She's already worked out a deal with the board," I said to Tella. "I saw Harding going into her house yesterday, and I suspect she was at the hunting lodge on Saturday. I heard the toilet flushing," I added, when Karen looked surprised. "Have you told your new husband exactly how close you are to Harding and Warfield?"

"Part of my value to Ted is my willingness to work with

the members of the board," Karen said calmly. "The board is very anxious to get back to business as usual. And frankly, Tella, they have no confidence in your management ability. They might even discourage any serious inquiries into your death, if it looks like an accident."

The helmet with Ted Scope's image moved in what may have been a nod.

"You're piling up too many bodies," I said. "Tella's right. It won't work."

"Then we'll try another approach. You pile up the bodies," Karen said. "You killed Chareese, you are going to shoot Tella, and then you are going to shoot yourself. How does that sound?"

"Unlikely," I told her.

"I'm afraid it will have to do." Karen took a gun out of her shoulder bag. "Ted, honey, Tella doesn't want to work for you anymore. We're going to have to let her go."

"You could still change your mind, Tella," the voice from the helmet said. "I'd like it if you'd stay and work for me, just the way you used to."

"We can talk about it, Mike. If you take off the helmet and tell your friend to put down the gun." Tella was the ice princess, in control again.

"I am Ted Scope, and Karen is my wife." Mike swiveled toward Karen. The field of vision inside the helmet had to be limited. "Ask Tella to work for us. We don't have to hurt her."

"She's already said no. I think we have to believe her." Karen moved forward next to Mike, so that both Tella and I were in easy range.

"Warfield is going to decide you're an embarrassment, Karen. He's going to cut you loose to take the rap, just the way he did with his Wall Street buddies," I said, hoping to shake her.

"I don't think so," she said.

"Think again," I said. "He hasn't done anything illegal here. If I'm right, he didn't even know about it when you decided to take a shot at Gloria after the graduation ceremony. You were acting on your own then and acting on your own when you shot Chareese. While everybody was wondering how the board was going to get rid of Gloria, Guy, and Tella, and keep Mike, you acted. It was in Warfield's interests—and Harding's, and Zabriskie's—to let Guy take the rap for Gloria's murder, especially if Tella could be implicated. But it wasn't Guy and Tella, was it?"

"No. The funny thing is that this started out as Gloria's idea. She liked the hologram in the pool, and she asked Mike if he wanted to dress up like his father. Gloria encouraged Mike to believe that he could take Ted's place. Tella, of course, would be out. Gloria said they could have a press conference and announce it. But when Ted here went out to talk with her beside the pool, she laughed at him. Ted didn't like it when she laughed at him." Karen threw a quick smile in the direction of the helmet.

"I pushed her in the water," the voice said. "I showed her I was the boss."

"You sure did, Ted, honey," Karen said. "Now we're going to show these two you're the boss."

"Guy thought you were the spaceman," Tella said. "He couldn't see the hologram from upstairs. He saw a blank helmet. Did you mean to frighten your brother?"

The helmet didn't react.

"And I don't understand why Chareese had to be killed," Tella added.

"Because she gave me away."

Karen's mouth became tight, her eyes dark and narrow. This new hardness erased the innocence from her face so thoroughly I couldn't understand how I had ever seen it there.

"How did you know?" I asked.

"Ted here set up a phone tap that fed all his family's conversations to an answering machine and gave me the remote code to pick them up. When I checked the machine Sunday morning, I decided to talk to Chareese myself, in person. I got her address from Ted's computer files and reached her condo just as she was leaving. I followed her to the park."

"But you couldn't have overheard our conversation," I said.

"No. Chareese was so certain I was harmless that she repeated it to me." Karen laughed, delighted with her own performance. The dark look was back almost at once. "She talked about me, after she had promised not to, because she thought Guy was innocent. I couldn't trust her any longer. I don't want anyone in the company who I can't trust to play on our team."

"I bet Warfield feels the same way," I said. "And he might not be too comfortable about the amount of stock you control as Mike's wife, with everyone else conveniently out of the way. I'd worry if I were you."

"I'm not worried. And you don't have to be much longer." She released the safety catch with her thumb—a thumb covered by a strip of flesh-colored adhesive.

"There's something else you have to worry about," I said. "You left evidence when you broke into Chareese's condo. Evidence you were there."

"Thank you for letting me know. I'll see about it later."

"What did you want in Chareese's condo?" Tella asked.

"Once I saw her, and the kind of car she was driving, I knew she had to have some kind of money. I thought maybe the guys were paying her on the side, but George—George Harding—said they weren't. That meant there was maybe another player involved. I had to check it out."

"What did you find?" I asked.

Karen laughed. "She must have inherited it. And that's enough about Chareese. Move over against the fireplace, both of you. "

"If you shoot us here, you'll have to shoot Beatriz, too," Tella said. "And I suspect that all this blood won't be good for Mike's productivity. What kind of leverage do you have if Mike's productivity slips? What happens to your deal? What do you think is left of the company if Mike can't work?"

"I'm Ted Scope," the voice said.

"Well, if you're really Ted Scope, then the company is in trouble," Tella said. "Because Ted Scope was burned out years ago. Ted's son Mike was the real genius."

"I'm Ted Scope. I'm in charge."

"You're in charge, Ted Scope. But you didn't invent a damned thing and you never will."

"I'm Ted Scope." The voice was strident, unnerved.

Karen frowned. Tella had done what I couldn't do. Tella had shaken her.

Karen looked at the smiling apparition next to her, and the barrel of the gun dropped slightly. The odds are against you when you rush someone with a gun—it's a heavy bet against the house—and I'd already done it once this week. My heart was pounding and my hands were sweaty. This was going to be my only chance to make a move.

The fireplace tools were only there for show, but they

were real brass. I grabbed the poker and threw it at Karen's head. Then I ducked down and lunged forward.

I heard the poker crack against something that wasn't a head. I connected with Karen's knees and felt her start to topple.

Then I heard three shots, and somebody was screaming.

I don't remember the rest.

Chapter
14

"HOW MANY FINGERS?"

I wasn't certain at first. They were too close, and they kept bobbing. I grabbed the hand and held it away from my face.

"Two."

"Who's President of the United States?"

"Promise me the answer isn't Dan Quayle. I already have a headache."

"She's okay."

That was Matthews's voice. I tried to lift myself to find out where he was, but a paramedic in scrubs—I think the same one who had held Chareese's knees—was blocking my view, and moving was hard on my head.

"Come on," the paramedic said. "I'll help you to the ambulance."

"No hospitals," I told him. "I don't like hospitals."

"You really ought to come with us," the paramedic said. "But since you're conscious, you have the right to refuse treatment."

"I refuse. Thanks for offering, though."

The paramedic moved out of the way, so that I could see the rest of the room. I was lying on the couch, the one I had left some time ago with the poker in my hand. Matthews was standing in front of the fireplace.

"Who's going to the hospital?" I asked.

"Mike Scope is going to the hospital. Flesh wound. Karen Hackstaff is going to the morgue."

"Tell me." I closed my eyes. My head hurt less that way.

"The poker cracked the helmet contraption, knocking Scope against Hackstaff, who shot him. The housekeeper shot Hackstaff. You got hit with the poker on its way down. Not hard, lucky for you. Just grazed your temple."

"I heard three shots."

"One hit the wall."

"Where's Tella?"

"I'm here," she said. "I'm fine. Thank you."

"For what? Thank Beatriz."

"You were willing to risk your life—you did risk your life—because you were convinced I needed help. Thank you for that. For believing I didn't plot to kill my mother. For understanding. For everything."

I opened my eyes and looked for her. She was sitting on the other couch.

"Okay. You're welcome."

"I gotta go, O'Neal," Matthews said. "Let me know when you can come in to make a formal statement. Tomorrow would be fine. In the meantime, take care of your head."

I struggled to sit, but Matthews was out the door. Once I got used to being upright, my head didn't feel too bad.

"Can I get you something?" Tella asked.

"Thanks. I could use another cup of tea."

"The tea's cold."

"That's okay."

I picked up the cup that I had put down however long ago it was. I was so thirsty I drank it all.

"They took Beatriz in," she said. "They won't charge her, will they?"

"I don't think so. I think taking her in was a formality."

"I didn't know she had a gun."

"Good thing she did."

Tella shivered.

"Are you going to be okay?" I asked.

"Of course. Eventually. I'm just not okay right now."

We sat there in silence. I was still trying to put together what had happened. Larry had been just evasive enough about his agent in the house that I thought I might be on my own. If I'd known Beatriz had a gun, I wouldn't have rushed Karen. And Mike might not have been shot. On the other hand, Tella wasn't hurt. Whatever else, I had taken care of my responsibility as I saw it. Or at least as Larry the Lamb had seen it.

"Do you want to go to the hospital to see about Mike?"

"Not right now. The paramedics said he'll be all right. And remember, he would have let that woman shoot me. I don't think I want to sit in a hall waiting to talk with him."

"Staying here by yourself isn't a good idea, either. Do you have anyone you could call—or anywhere you'd like to go?"

"I can't think of anyone. But you're welcome to stay here as long as you want," she said. "I have plenty of room."

She even managed a laugh.

"I can't sleep well without my cats," I told her. "In any case, I have a better idea. Where's your computer?"

"My office—it's next to my bedroom."

"I can make it to the other wing." I stood up, hoping I hadn't lied.

We walked down the hall, across the Oriental rug, past the martyred saint. Tella opened the door to a room with a sunny view of the yard and the pool, a far more cheerful room than her office at Scope Chips. She gestured toward a terminal on a heavy mahogany desk.

"Do me a favor," I said. "Boot it up and connect to Internet."

She did as told, then moved out of the way.

If Larry the Lamb's address had been complicated, I never could have remembered it. But it wasn't, and the headache hadn't killed my memory of the discussion.

"This may take a while," I said. "Could I have some hot tea and a couple of aspirin?"

Tella left, and I started typing. She interrupted briefly to give me the aspirin, and I shooed her away until I was finished.

I brought Larry up to date on the events of the afternoon. Then I told him I thought he'd made a mistake by letting Tella think Scope was her father. My guess was that Scope had somehow figured he wasn't, and it had affected his relationships with everybody in the family, especially Tella. But whether it was a mistake or not, everything was different now. Ted and Gloria were both gone, Mike and Guy were both nuts, and Tella needed somebody to care about her. I added that he had an hour to make a move. After that I was going to tell her what I knew.

My headache was bad enough that I wouldn't even have minded if he'd shot me. At least it would have ended the pain. The aspirin had barely made a dent.

"Do you want tea in here?" Tella asked from the doorway.

"Sure. I don't think the answer will be E-mail, but we might as well see."

"See what?"

"What happens in an hour."

She disappeared again and returned almost immediately

with the tray from the library. The blueberry muffins were still untouched. The water was hot again, though.

We couldn't seem to get a conversation going. When the phone rang, we were both startled, as if we had been sitting in a trance.

"It's for you," she said, handing it to me.

"I'm afraid it'll take me two hours to get there, Miss O'Neal. Do you think you can wait that long?" Larry Agnotti said.

"See you then."

I hung up the phone.

"Who was that?" Tella asked.

"Someone I want you to meet."

"This just isn't the time."

"Yes, it is. You're going to have to trust me on this one."

She scrutinized me carefully, as if she still hadn't made a decision on my character.

"You are aware, aren't you, that my life has been destroyed. Not just my brother, not just the company, but my whole life. I don't have a reason to get up in the morning. And I don't feel like being polite to a stranger."

"Then throw him out when he gets here. But this is the time to meet him. I have a reason."

"All right. But it better be good."

I hoped it was.

Tella scrounged up some soup from the kitchen, to go with the blueberry muffins. I was glad she didn't want to rehash everything. I think she was glad I didn't want to.

We were back to silence when the doorbell rang.

And I was ready to go home.

Someone else would have stayed for the scene, I know that. Someone else would have wanted to know what he said, what she said, how Tella reacted when she found out the good news—somebody cared—and the bad news—she couldn't show him off in public.

But I wasn't up for all that, and I didn't figure it was any of my business. They could let me know what they wanted me to know.

I did wonder what she was going to do, though, faced with the choice of a crazy family or a crooked one. And even that wasn't clear cut. I hadn't known Ted Scope, but I had met his pals. The difference between Larry Agnotti and Tom Warfield was one of degree, not of kind, and Larry was in his way a more caring father than Ted Scope.

I got home too tired to do anything but take two more aspirin and go to bed. I slept for sixteen hours, in fact.

The sleep took care of the headache, if not the bruise on the side of my face. The first item on my agenda the next day was cleaning my office—really cleaning it, not just moving paper around. I had to make sure that there were no missed communications devices. Once I'd done it, I kind of liked the way things looked.

I started cleaning the rest of the house.

Sandra called, annoyed again because I hadn't given her a call before the police reporter got the story. I promised to meet her for lunch and fill in anything he had missed. Ramona called, annoyed because I hadn't warned her—and Al—that my name would be in the newspapers.

I was about to wander over to the Mother Lode for dinner, knowing that Deke would be annoyed because I hadn't shown up the night before to let him know I was all right, when I remembered that I had never returned Curtis Breckinridge's phone call from Sunday. I picked up the phone.

"I got an E-mail message," I said. "Just wondered if you can tell me anything about the sender."

I gave him Larry the Lamb's address.

"Not a thing," he said. "Why are you asking?"

I was asking because the river of my paranoia had overflowed its banks, and for one brief moment anyone who used Internet and had known either Gloria or Tella was suspect.

"Just curious," was all I said.

"I read about your case in this morning's paper. Are they all that exciting?"

"Fortunately, no. But I'd be happy to tell you about some of them. How about dinner tomorrow?"

"Fine," he said. His voice lifted. I liked the way his voice lifted when he talked to me. "That would be fine."

I walked to the Mother Lode with a light step, looking up as the clear, indigo sky gave way to a neon haze.

Deke was annoyed, but he got over it.

I lost two games of Keno and decided not to play again that evening. I had something to look forward to, after all.